Golden Nuggets

Treasures from 50 Years of the Cisco Writers Club
1975-2025

Edited by Priscilla Bettis

Cisco Writers Club
Cisco, Texas

Golden Nuggets: Treasures from 50 Years of the Cisco Writers Club, 1975–2025

ISBN: 978-1-962898-04-1
First Edition: October 2015

Edited by Priscilla Bettis
Cover Image © Anton Matyukha / DepositPhotos — used with permission
Interior and Cover Design by Kadesh Ink Author Services & Raena St. Peter
ISBN donated by Ithirial Rising Press

Printed in the United States of America

This anthology is dedicated to the past, present, and future members of the Cisco Writers Club and to every storyteller, poet, and dreamer who has shared their words and hearts to nurture the creative spirit.

Our heartfelt gratitude also goes to the contributing authors for their generosity in supporting this project. Your voices remind us that stories endure, inspire, and unite us.

May this collection stand as a celebration of the power of words and the enduring legacy of those who write them.

Table of Contents

THE ROCK

An Inspirational Short Story by Linda Gordon

In the beginning God created the heavens and the earth. The earth was formless and empty, and darkness covered the deep waters. And the Spirit of God was hovering over the surface of the waters. Then God said, "Let there be light," and there was light. And God saw that the light was good. Then he separated the light from the darkness. God called the light "day" and the darkness "night." And evening passed and morning came, marking the first day. Then God said, "Let there be a space between the waters, to separate the waters of the heavens from the waters of the earth." And that is what happened. God made this space to separate the waters of the earth from the waters of the heavens. God called the space "sky." And evening passed and morning came, marking the second day. Then God said, "Let the waters beneath the sky flow together into one place, so dry ground may appear." And that is what happened. God called the dry ground "land" and the waters "seas." And God saw that it was good. (Genesis 1:1-10 NLT)

"That's me," thought the rock buried deep in the earth, newly formed, newly born as the creation called "land." It was only the third day, and God had more creating to do, but it did not concern the rock. He was buried deep underground and could not see what came after, but he was overjoyed to know that the Great Creator chose him for this task. Only water, light, and sky had been created before him, so he considered himself fourth in the scheme of Creation, a lofty place to be. He reveled in his strength and his size, stretching out beyond sight. He knew the Creator had a purpose for everything, and in his mind, it was easy to see what his purpose would be. He was meant to support all that was created after him. He was even given the job of containing and guiding the water that flowed through him in accordance with the Divine plan for this place called Earth.

Many days passed, and the rock spent his time proudly fulfilling his purpose, secure in his strength and position. He often thought about the service he was providing and hoped that whatever he was supporting would consider whom to thank for this job.

Then, one day, the rock heard a rumbling deep inside of the earth, and he felt the first crack, the first fissure of separation from his lofty position, the thing that he prized the most. The rock cried out as he felt himself slipping, but there was nothing that he could have done. The land was pushed together with the mightiest of hands, and the two halves split upwards and apart, breaking the rock away from its mooring and throwing him out of the huge crack in the earth. He landed on the ground a short distance away, where he lay still and dazed at his sudden misfortune.

When the tremors finally subsided, the rock looked around and was surprised and dismayed to discover that he was much smaller than before, an infinitely smaller fraction of his former self. He had not realized that he was not the whole of the land God created, but just a piece of an expanse joined in unity of purpose, seamlessly meshed together. He felt lost and even smaller lying in the sparse vegetation that still managed to hinder his vision in this alien new circumstance.

At first, the rock felt frightened. It was all new and so strange, but nothing else harmed him as he lay under the grass. He had plenty of time to think during the years that he lay there, warmed by the sun and cooled by the night that had been created so long ago. "They still have their purpose," he often thought, and he mourned for his own lost place in Creation. But as time went on, he began to realize that even though he had been secure in his certainty that he was supporting the world, it had been a dark and silent place, deep in the earth, and he began to notice things around him. Like the way the grass where he lay changed with each season, greener at times, dry brown at others, or the way the wind whistled softly through it when it was green and rustled loudly when it was brown. He grew accustomed to the breath of the wind blowing over him and welcomed its touch in the heat. The great crack in the earth had created a new pathway for water to flow. The rock noticed the soft song of the river when the water was low and the loud roaring torrent when the rains came and washed quickly through the crevice, tumbling over itself in its hurry. Over time, the rock grew to welcome the sights and sounds of the insects and reptiles that lived beside him and on him, and he was almost content for a time.

Finally, after many years, sheep came to this land, chewing the grass to ground as they grazed, exposing the rock for the first time. From this new view point, the rock watched a young shepherd as he tended his sheep. He was patient and gentle with his flock and often brought his sheep to the river to drink. Some days the boy lingered on the river bank, and the rock watched intently as he gathered smooth stones to put in his pouch. "What purpose could there be for a rock smaller than I am?" he wondered. It wasn't until later that he saw the young boy take his leather sling and a stone and kill a lion stalking his sheep. A new hope bloomed in the rock that he could once again have a purpose that he could define, if only the boy would choose him. Each time the boy came to the river to gather his stones, the rock silently pleaded to be one of those stones that flew straight and true in defense of the helpless sheep. Finally, one day, the young boy came to choose stones, taking his time, weighing each in his hand. The rock knew there must be a special purpose for these stones, so carefully were they selected. The rock counted, the boy would pick five, that's what his pouch would hold. He held his breath as the boy put the fourth in his pouch, then reached for the rock that had lain for so long after being spit out of the earth. At first his heart sang, until he felt the boy rubbing his hands over the rough and jagged places left from where he had been torn loose from the land. The rock knew then that the sling would not be his purpose after all. The boy drew his arm back and the rock flew through the air and then landed in the water, sinking to the bottom in utter despair.

The rock lay, uncaring, for uncharted time. Disappointment lay heavy, weighing him down, so that the waters washed over him, unnoticed, unheeded, day after day. Time passed, and as the water stroked him over and over, he began to let go of his anger and sadness. He noticed with surprise that the rough edges on him had been eroded and smoothed away over time as well, and he had been rounded into a rock perfect for a sling. He briefly thought of what might have been, but as the rock lay in the midst of the water, the first of creation, sustenance for all living things, he began to feel a peace unlike any he had known before.

He gave himself up to the peace he was feeling, and he found himself delighting in the smallest of things. The flash of the sun on the fin of a fish, the prisms of color he momentarily glimpsed, the froth of the foam as it eddied around him. He noticed other things, too, like how small he was getting, sloughing away with each caress of the water. The rock had much time to be thinking on things, and the initial panic he had felt had been gone a long time. He could only think on the things that he knew, which were limited at best, but he had lived under the earth, on the land, and now in the water for long periods of time. So he thought of those things and tried to understand the Grand Plan and find his place in that plan. Try as he might, he couldn't figure it out, so he just gave himself up to the way things were going. It felt good to just go with the flow. Then came the day that the last piece of rock fell apart, crumbling into particles of silt and floating down to become part of the mud at the bottom of the river. "So this is it," thought the rock, with momentary regret. "The once mighty rock is now just specks in the mud, humbled and lowly, no hope for a future beyond this."

"I don't care," thought the rock, with sudden joy in his heart. "I have all that I need here, what more could I want?" And he thanked the Creator for that insight.

No sooner had the rock finished his thanksgiving thought than he felt a disturbance in the water downstream. It was a fisherman coming, as they occasionally did, wading through the current, casting his line. A shadow hovered overhead as a boot blocked the light, and then down, down it came into the mud. The rock was instantly pressed into a crevice and lifted up as the boot took a step. He was lifted twice more before reaching the bank. The shock of the air after being in the water so long was disorienting, and it took a minute for the rock to realize that he had stopped. The fisherman was gone, and the rock saw that he lay alone on the bank, formed into a pattern of tread. Dry land felt very strange after such a long time. Even the vegetation was different than he remembered, having been carried downstream over time. Just then a butterfly came to rest on a vivid flower close by. Distracted by its beauty, the rock could only stare, entranced by the delicate wings.

"This is even better!" thought the rock, "so much beauty to see." His heart sang with thanks for this unexpected gift, but the Creator of all was not done with him yet. He sent His sun to dry out the mud, pressed into a mold by the sole of a boot. It wasn't long before the heat did its work, and the rock crumbled again, not into silt, but into a fine, dry pile of dust.

The rock now felt almost weightless, no cares pressing down, but a question kept burning in the back of his mind. When the wind came to get him, the rock couldn't help asking the Creator, "Please, will you tell me my purpose in your Divine plan?"

As the wind lifted and twirled the dust high into the sky, the rock heard a soft voice over the roar.

"Your purpose all along, my precious creation, was just to submit to My plan."

Then the wind turned the rock loose, and the particles were scattered in every direction to see wonders beyond anything he could imagine. The heavy, hard rock, brought out of cold darkness, had been patiently transformed into specks held aloft in the breeze. Without any pride or uncertainty or regret left to weigh him down, the rock had finally been set joyously free.

VOWS BENEATH A HARVEST MOON

A Short Story by Ruth V. York

Otto clicked the "Create Mail" button and slowly began the same words he had typed almost daily for sixty-five years: "My dearest Mary..."

How many more? he wondered. How many more days, begun with this simple phrase? His doctors didn't know, but they had warned him afresh to set his house in order.

As if Otto hadn't lived with Death as a companion for most of his ninety years.

It had started well before the chilly October night when the soldiers' rifle butts crashed against the door of the apartment house, filling the street below with their thunderous boots. But remembering that night was glorious, thrilling, unlike the years of crippling illness that had kept him almost wholly confined to his rooms.

He thought of the shattered German village he had known all his life, stark under a luminous harvest moon. The artillery rumbling ever nearer, bringing the ebbing struggle of the Nazi war machine to his tiny world.

He saw Mary Schultz's terror-filled eyes as she entered the dark room with his nephew clutched in her arms. She had been a faithful attendant and housekeeper for the two of them despite the daily perils and glamorous opportunities that had lured away her predecessor.

"Herr Krackit, what will we do?" she had whispered.

"Take Joseph. The money in the hidden wall safe, and the diamonds. And his mother's picture, Mary. Go to the village priest. I've talked to him. He'll get you both safely to Switzerland."

She dragged a gasping breath. This village was all she had known. To take a child, alone, into the broken, shattered, insane world? She was but sixteen, and frightened.

"But Joseph ... it's not right. He should have you, family, someone to look after him."

Otto touched her elbow gently. "Mary, look at me. You mean more to him than anyone, since his mother is gone. I can't help him now, only if you will do this thing for me. It's dangerous, I know, but I fear staying is more so. Will you do it?"

She hesitated, wild-eyed. "But I'm not—I'm just a—a—Herr Krackit, you know I can never be a proper mother to him."

He knew what she was thinking. Her mother's house, barely earning the name. Her mother's unsavory standing in the community, her own humiliation there. Until, that is, she had come to work for Herr Krackit and little Joseph.

He took both her elbows now, willing her to meet his eyes. To close out the tumult at the front door. To pour strength and his trust into her very soul.

"Marry me, Mary. Then you'll be family. Perhaps all the family he has. Go to Father Rudolph tonight. Tell him we got married and to register it in the parish book. Tell him to get both of you safely to Switzerland. Take Joseph to America if you can. Start a new life. For him, and my sister. For me. And don't worry. I'll be all right."

He remembered her eyes, impossibly wide in the soft light from the window, as she had whispered, "I, Mary Schultz, take thee, Herr—*Otto*—Krackit ..." And then, with the soldiers pounding up the stairs, she had slipped through the window, Joseph in her arms, and down the rickety iron fire escape.

"I am well enough," Otto tapped out slowly. "Thank you for the pictures of Joseph's new grandson. Such a handsome lad. Tell him the story, Mary. He needs to hear it all, and often. He needs to know what a heroine his Great Aunt Mary is.

"Yours forever, Otto."

HURRY EVERY CHANCE YOU GET

A Memoir Essay by Priscilla Bettis

Daddy died last month. He was eighty-eight.

He often said, "Hurry every chance you get." I'd forget my coat on the way to the car on a chilly, winter morning and have to run inside to get it. Glancing at his watch, he'd call after me, "Hurry every chance you get." But it wasn't strictly about time. He said it to the neighbors as they left for a mid-summer trip to visit family in Oklahoma. "Hope the weather's good for you all, and hurry every chance you get."

Before heading out to trick-or-treat with a friend, sitting for a ninth-grade history midterm, or taking my first lesson with the driving instructor: "Hurry every chance you get."

You'd think Daddy was a Type A personality with all that *hurry* in him. (By the way, it was never *Mom* and *Dad*. It was always *Mother* and *Daddy*. Maybe that's a Southern thing, me being a third-generation Texan.) But no. He knew how to lie in the grass and watch clouds float by. He knew how to enjoy fishing when the fish weren't biting. Daddy could have just as easily said, "Focus on what matters, and don't waste energy on all that other stuff."

Don't fiddle around picking a coat. Just grab one.

Enjoy your trip to Oklahoma.

You two kids be safe trick-or-treating.

You've studied thoroughly for the midterm.

You'll do fine behind the wheel.

Apparently, Daddy said the same thing at work. One year his fellow petroleum engineers got together and gave him a plaque engraved with *Hurry every chance you get*. I rescued the chipped, scratched plaque from the toss pile at my parents' longtime abode before Mother listed the property and moved to senior housing to start her widowhood.

I'm not all that sad at Daddy's passing because I've already grieved. He had Alzheimer's, and he stopped recognizing me in 2018. I realized the father I knew was gone. I shed tears for two years and punched pillows and screamed at God and did all the typical things grieving people do. Daddy's recent corporeal death is a relief, really, a relief that his clever and kind and wonderful mind is finally free of that awful disease.

Because Alzheimer's sucks.

The last time Daddy and I had a conversation when he still recognized me, we were walking on the sidewalk outside the hospital. Actually, I was walking. He had trouble with his gait by then and was shuffling. He was trying to describe what was going on in his head and getting more agitated with every word. He said he could "see" chunks of his brain go black.

"I know, Daddy. That's why you're under the care of several doctors."

"Do they have a diagnosis?"

Do I tell him? I didn't know if it would upset him to tell him his diagnosis or if he'd get even more frustrated not knowing. This was new territory for me. Over the next few steps (shuffles) I remembered the honest things he had shared with me over the years, uncomfortable things about why a family member had such a short temper, why another relative always did that *thing*, and even what happened to the neighbor boy in the pond.

"You have Alzheimer's," I said.

His masculine, adult veneer cracked. "Then people will make fun of me," he whined. I had *never* heard my dad whine, but I knew the disease did awful things to a victim's personality.

"No they won't," I said. "I won't let them." His shoe was untied. He couldn't tie a shoe anymore, so I knelt and tied it for him.

"How will you stop them?" His normal voice again.

"I'll beat 'em up!" I stood and swung a fist through the air to punctuate my promise.

Daddy laughed. It was the same laugh he used years ago when my junior high friends and I would be up to some antic or another, as in, *Oh, you silly kids.*

It didn't matter that I had told him his diagnosis. By the time the sidewalk ended and we were at the doors to the hospital, the part of his brain that stored me, that remembered conversations, that understood diagnoses, was black.

It may not have made me particularly sad when Daddy passed away, but it threw me off kilter. Like God had taken the horizon and tilted it. I stumbled around. *What do I do next? Why can't I think in a straight line?*

I set up a mini-memorial with his picture, a candle, and the old plaque I had rescued. Every time I sit down to write I light the candle. Daddy is my writing muse for now. He reminds me to keep moving forward, to hurry every chance I get.

OF THOSE DEAD

An excerpt from the novel *Of Those Dead* by Brian Callarman

Chapter 2

Water Snake Girl

The Texas Republic, East of the Llano Estacado, 1835

Water Snake Girl struggled against the cords that bound her hands. They were tight, and she had been bound for days. Things hadn't started out that way. At the outset of the journey her captors hadn't been quite so harsh. They hadn't expected her to cause any trouble. She was, after all, a young girl and just as much their dependent as their captive in an unfamiliar and hostile country.

The fire crackled, a freshly skinned jackrabbit roasting over it. From a nearby mesquite, a mourning dove wept, cooing its despondent song to the rising sun. An errant gust caressed Water Snake Girl's raven hair and brought with it the scent of the roasting hare; her stomach growled, her mouth watered. She had the fleeting thought that this would be a pleasant morning; would be, if not for the six Kiowa warriors sauntering about the camp preparing for another day of hard riding through a boundless, dry plain filled with jagged rocks and stinging insects and thorns.

They had been moving with a purpose, a destination in mind, but other than *south* she hadn't been able to discern what it might be. The language her captors spoke was as unfamiliar to her as the landscape she now found herself in. Parts of their speech were recognizable: gestures, inflections, a few phrases; but she could only gather bits and snatches of what they said to one another and to her. Due to that, their terminus had remained largely obscure, except that it had to do with some fashion of traders; *Comancheros* they were called, who she understood wouldn't be at some unnamed rendezvous much longer.

Water Snake Girl wriggled a finger into the thongs about her wrists. She pulled, hoping for some relief on a spot that had become badly chaffed. This elicited a harsh look from one of the older men in the group. He glared at her with hard, dark eyes and made a motion as if he were going to come over to where she was. Water Snake Girl ceased her struggling. He went back to tending the rabbit.

It seemed like an age had lumbered past since her life had taken this dreadful turn, but it had only been about two turnings of the moon since she and her brother were captured from their village on the banks of the Great River. Water Snake Girl wasn't old enough to understand the nuances of inter-tribal relations, but her people, the Pawnee, had always spoken of the Kiowa with nothing less than bitter contempt. Now she understood why. A Kiowa raiding party had sneaked into their camp in the dark, snatched several children and some horses, and fought unpityingly with the men who tried to intervene. Her father had been one of those. He charged out of his lodge, musket in hand, and shot a Kiowa off his pony. Unfortunately, another warrior he'd failed to see in the fracas rode up from behind and ran a plains lance through him.

It made her sad to think of her father. He had been a strong man in life, a proud warrior with eighteen Oglala coups to his credit, a respected buffalo hunter, but she was certain the Kiowa lance had been his end. It also made her sad to think about her older brother, Two Crows. In the days following their capture, the war party had taken the children, eight in all, back to a camp where lots of trading had been going on. The Kiowa had been hard on Water Snake Girl and her brother. They were both beaten multiple times for seemingly no other purpose except their captors had a mind to do so. She had also been violated, roughly, by a pubescent boy in the camp; an altogether horrific experience made worse by the fact that it had been done in full view of her brother. Of all the things that had happened to them—being captured, their father being killed, the beatings—this was the event that affected Two Crows the most. His eyes changed after that, his hatred for the Kiowa blazing like a hundred suns. Both of them were children, but her brother was older and already had much of the warrior spirit in him. Water Snake Girl had worried about him. She feared his consuming odium would drive him to do something rash and he would get himself killed. Life among the Kiowa was hardly bearable, but she still wanted her brother to live.

Whether Two Crows would end up doing something rash was not something Water Snake Girl was destined to see in the end. After some days with the Kiowa, a large group of Comanche arrived at the camp. These were strange, hard, swarthy people; much like the Kiowa in manner, but somehow more leathery, more lean and fierce. They wore no frills or feathers, just black paint and buffalo-horned caps. Some of the older warriors wore garments whose seams were stitched with human hair, presumably from enemies they'd bested and scalped.

When the Comanche arrived, a couple days of revelry ensued. A cache of whiskey was delved into, and men feasted on all sorts of game and gambled for a sundry of items. As the festivities wound down, the men started bartering for various trade items: muskets, blankets, knives, buffalo robes, decorative articles, horses, and the captive Pawnee children. There had been a great deal of discussion between several of the Comanche and her Kiowa abductors about Water Snake Girl. The man they called Kills On Top seemed most interested. Ultimately, a price was agreed upon, and the Kiowa traded her for six Comanche ponies. She never got the chance to say goodbye to her brother. Kills On Top hefted her onto his mare, and he and thirty other Comanche warriors bid farewell to their friends and cantered away.

The trail had been a long one; the Comanche were tireless riders, scarcely stopping for water and food, and when they did, it was all business. They slaked their need and rode on. Like ripples upon the water the days rolled past, and with it the scenery changed around them.

Prairie became undulating hills and oaks; hills became brush and coulees; brush and coulees became plains, and the plains grew dryer by the day, by the step. It seemed to Water Snake Girl that all the plants in this accursed country had thorns and wished for nothing less than to stick them into her flesh.

At length, the party of travelers came to a small river, a reddish trickle meandering through an over-sized gorge, where they settled in and rested for four days. Some of the men hunted to replenish their provisions, but mostly they spent the time resting, telling stories, and gambling. Intermittent grassy fields provided nearby graze for the horses to refresh themselves as well. The Comanche men regarded Water Snake Girl very little during that time, although she was fed well and not mistreated. Through quiet observation, she found she was becoming more familiar with her new captors as individuals. She had learned some of their names, and although their language was largely foreign to her, she could tell that a conversation occasionally broke out about her. Kills On Top would gesture about his face and say the word she understood to mean, *lovely—like the rising sun.* Others would nod their heads in agreement. As the conversation proceeded, other words commonly used were things she understood to mean *fresh ... valuable ... good for trade*, as well as *Comancheros who would not be* somewhere *much longer.*

Water Snake Girl was beginning to understand her new place in the world. She was no longer a young girl, treasured by her family, learning from her grandmother to tan hides, gather edible plants, and live and make life in a Pawnee village, hoping to fall in love and marry a Pawnee brave someday; she had become a trade item. Perhaps a valuable trade item, but still nothing more than an object to be placed on a blanket along with so many tools and trinkets and bartered for.

Four horses and I keep the Pawnee girl.

No, plainly you can see she is worth more than that, seven.

I will give you five.

I will take six horses and no less.

We are agreed, then. Six horses, and I may take her south to the land of thorns and stinging insects.

Agreed.

She was coming to understand this new cruelty, and she resented it with her every fiber.

She had hated the Kiowa for their rough treatment of her and the other children, but they had also terrified her into submission. The Comanche were a fearsome lot in their own right, but her resentment against them for the simple act of trading horses for her was beginning to out-blaze the fear of the brutality they too were undoubtedly capable of.

As the Comanche men were concluding their hiatus at the river, there was a lengthy discussion. Water Snake Girl deduced the party was about to separate. Some of them were from a different band than others. It also seemed Kills On Top was intent on continuing south, with his valuable item. Most of the other men were cautioning him against the route he intended. *The Devil lives there,* a couple of them said. Some actively tried to talk him out of his plans, others appeared willing to go with him out of loyalty or an opportunity for adventure and renown. *I rode with Kills On Top through the Devil's home*. Still others sat by, drawing in the dust with a finger, not inclined to show any particular opinion in the matter.

The Devil ... that phrase again.

Kills On Top made an animated gesture of dismissal. *A man ... shoot arrows into him ... dead man.*

Most of the party seemed dubious of this assertion.

More discussion ensued and Kills On Top went back to a phrase that was now becoming familiar to Water Snake Girl: *Comancheros ... leaving soon*.

At length, an agreement was reached among the men; however, the specifics of that agreement remained elusive to their young captive. The Comanches collected their horses and provisions and bade farewell to one another. The bulk of the party trotted away west, while Kills On Top and five intrepid bucks splashed through the red-colored water, carrying Water Snake Girl with them south.

Her loathing of the Comanche festered deeper with each passing day, with each turn in the trail, with each gully, each cactus and rock. Six horses—that's what she was worth. The grueling ride wore on. The hostile nature of the landscape increased with every footfall.

Water Snake Girl had thought the Comanche were hard riders in a larger group, but riding in a small party of six hardened braves was an assault on the senses. Although they seemed to be holding up, she pitied their horses, feeling kindred to them at some level; she had been traded for some of their brethren after all. She also felt sorry for herself and enjoyed imagining what her father would do to these men when he encountered them in the next world, in the land of the sky people.

Their rest stops were infrequent as water was scarce; at one point in the journey, they went for two complete days without water. No one complained; they just plodded on with their ponies frothing at the mouth from thirst. At length, a row of live oaks appeared on the horizon. The men shouted for joy and pointed with enthusiasm. This jubilant commotion from her usually stoic captors was quite a surprise. They leaned into their mounts and kicked them into a brisk gallop, whooping in their high-pitched Comanche style.

As the trees she'd seen at a distance drew near, Water Snake Girl saw what the men were excited about; a large spring of fresh water bubbled out of the ground. They leaped from their mounts and dove to their hands and knees; they drank deeply. Water Snake Girl and the horses did the same. That was the end of the day's ride. Even though it was early afternoon, they went ahead and made camp at the spring. The Comanche men never appeared to get tired, at least not that she'd been able to tell, but for the rest of the day they all were content to lounge about and enjoy the shade provided by the expansive live oaks growing there. The horses were unhaltered and released to munch the abundant grass of the little oasis.

The afternoon was hot, and Water Snake Girl had taken refuge on a blanket under the shade of a sprawling tree. She drifted off to sleep only to dream about continuing to ride through this menacing land where all the plants had thorns and all the insects stung or bit. In the dream she found herself right back on Kills On Top's pony, continuing her march toward eternity.

It was not a restful sleep, but Water Snake Girl was quite annoyed when awakened by a full bladder and a desperate need to relieve herself. She rolled off her blanket, stood, and started for some nearby brush for a little privacy. As she did, one of the men, a younger buck she understood to be called Red Dog, barked an order at her of which she didn't catch a word. She didn't say anything in return, hadn't understood what he'd said anyway, and just returned his guttural vocalization with a glare. Water Snake Girl was finding it increasingly difficult to hide her disdain for these men. She turned back toward the brush and proceeded. Red Dog repeated his command, or question, a little more forcefully this time and rose to his feet.

"I need to urinate, you horse's anus!" she snapped at him in Pawnee and continued on her quest for relief.

Likewise, Red Dog understood nothing of what she had said, nothing except *horse's anus*. He covered the distance between the two of them in a fraction of a moment and caught Water Snake Girl by the hair. She gasped with pain as he yanked her to her knees. In a loud voice, Red Dog proceeded to fire off a lecture on how a captive of the Comanche must behave—or else; he patted the large tomahawk hanging from his belt to drive home his meaning. The exchange garnered the attention of the others who all looked up from what they had been doing. With a violent shove, Red Dog released Water Snake Girl's hair and motioned toward the brush for her to proceed. She did, and he followed her.

Water Snake Girl found a suitable spot, but she hesitated to squat and do her business as Red Dog was still standing there, glowering over her, making it clear he intended to watch. As if the indignity of being traded for horses wasn't enough, she now had to urinate with this dolt watching after he had just pulled her hair and shouted at her. Infuriated, Water Snake Girl was about to do something rash.

"Will you at least turn around?" she asked in Pawnee.

Red Dog cocked his head and sneered without understanding.

Turn. She knew that word in the Comanche tongue. She made a circular motion with her finger as she said it.

Red Dog looked her up and down wearing a nasty smirk. With a smug grunt, he granted her request for a moment of privacy and turned his back. Water Snake Girl squatted and the blessed relief came, but she kept her eyes trained on the back of Red Dog's head. As she completed her task, she quietly scooped up a handful of sand.

She finished and stood again. Red Dog, still smirking, turned back to face her. As he did, he received a ration of sand in the eyes as Water Snake Girl flung the contents of her hand with all her might. She wheeled and ran.

Water Snake Girl ran as fast as her young legs would carry her, angry shouts erupting from behind. She didn't know where she was going. She had no plan. She had just acted out of anger and defiance and was now running toward the miles of dry country where she would have only thorns and snakes and stinging insects for companions—all were better than the Comanche. Onward the girl sprinted, but her flight was destined to be short-lived. She leaped over a spiny cactus and one of the men was already upon her, the one called Spotted Tail.

Spotted Tail was one of the older men of the group, but remarkably fleet-footed. He ran up behind her and knocked her to the ground with a violent, two-handed shove. Her head whipped backward from the force of the blow causing her neck to smart, the rocky ground biting into her knees. She rolled over a patch of thorns that embedded in her arm and side. Her flight coming to an end, she looked up to see Red Dog rubbing his eyes and swearing in his language. He kicked her several times and roared obscenities. He stopped long enough to rub his eyes once more and glowered down at the cowering girl. With a furious snarl, he drew the tomahawk from his belt and seemed intent on splitting her head with it.

Water Snake Girl's defiance wavered as the men crowded around her. She tried to force herself to glare back at them, but for a small girl lying on the rocky ground, being surrounded by hardened Comanche warriors was an intimidating proposition by any measure. Her eyes found those of Red Dog into which she had recently flung a handful of grit. She suddenly became quite terrified of what he might do with that tomahawk he now gripped at the ready. In truth, this may have been all Red Dog was actually intending, to terrify her back into submission the way the Kiowa had done, but his people were certainly not known for their restraint when angry. Whatever his true intentions may have been, the girl was convinced he would have buried the knapped flint blade between her eyes if it hadn't been for Kills On Top's intervention.

Kills On Top and Red Dog exchanged words of which Water Snake Girl understood nothing. Red Dog gestured about wildly with the tomahawk still in hand. Kills On Top's alien words were direct, calculated, and deliberate. He didn't seem as angry about her ridiculous escape attempt as he was concerned about protecting his investment. After a brief conversation between the two men, Red Dog looked at her again for one last intimidating glower. He then spat out a final denigrating epithet and stormed away in a dramatic huff. Kills On Top watched him go. Red Dog may have disagreed with keeping the girl's head in one piece, but it was evident Kills On Top was a respected leader among his people, and his word won out.

Red Dog stomped back to the spring to splash water in his reddened eyes. Kills On Top, with a stern visage, knelt beside Water Snake Girl. Taking both of her small wrists in one hand, he produced a leather thong and bound them tightly together. After he finished, he stuck a chastising finger in her face and said, *stupid girl ... stupid girl ...* He then followed up with a brief lecture that Water Snake Girl understood to mean, *next time I will not save you.*

DUST AND STONES

Steve Denehan

Not quite dead, nowhere near alive
he lies forward
splayed on his horse
his face in her mane
his arms hanging limply
either side of her neck

not an outlaw, barely a cowboy
soon to be nineteen
his father's son
the apple of his mother's eye
in town for salt and coffee grounds
to catch a bee-sting bullet

he does not remember the robbery
the young men, hats low, faces scarved
riding hard and shooting wildly
the lawmen giving chase
he does not remember
much of anything

he watched the chestnut shoulder
white knee
yellow ground
the dust and stones
jumping with each step
as tiny detonations

he watched tufts of grass
dock leaves and dog daisies
pass by in stop motion
until his eyelids
turned to lead and everything
became dark

he wonders
if he has always been on this horse
if that pale white hand, red-streaked
is his hand
if this is death
if the pain is over, or yet to come

he does not know
if the distant voice
is real or of his own creation
he knows only
that it is his mother, and that
it is getting closer

TWO THINGS REVEALED IN EXODUS

An Inspirational Article by J.V. Lewis

The first thing I want to call attention to is how we know that Mount Horeb and Mount Sinai are one and the same.

"Now Moses was pasturing the flock of Jethro his father-in-law, the priest of Midian; and led his flock to the west side of the wilderness and came to Horeb, the mountain of God" (Exodus 3:1). God tells Moses, "[W]hen you have brought the people out of Egypt, you shall worship God at this mountain" (Exodus 3:12b NASB). After the Children of Israel had left Egypt, they came "to the wilderness of Sinai and camped in the wilderness; and there Israel camped in front of the mountain" (Exodus 19:2b NASB).

So we see that the mountain of Sinai in Exodus 19 is the same as the mountain of Horeb in Exodus 3.

The second thing I want to draw attention to is that the Angel of the Lord is also the Lord, the God of Abraham, Isaac, and Jacob. For that, let's begin with Exodus 3 when the angel of the Lord appeared to Moses in a burning bush: "*The angel of the Lord* appeared to him in a blazing fire from the midst of a bush; and he looked, and behold, the bush was burning with fire, yet the bush was not consumed. So Moses said, 'I must turn aside now and see this marvelous sight, why the bush is not burned up.' When the *Lord* saw that he turned aside to look, *God* called to him from the midst of the bush" (Exodus 3:2-4a NASB).

The question is, was it the Angel of the Lord, the Lord, or God? Of course, the answer is YES to all! God was there in the burning bush.

A little farther down in the same chapter, God specifies that he *is "the God of Abraham, the God of Isaac, and the God of Jacob"* (Exodus 3:6a NASB).

While these things are not the thrust of the main subject of Exodus, I hope you find them to be points of interest as I do. The work of Michael Heiser has caused me to be alert and notice passages such as these. Other similarities can be found throughout the Old Testament.

THE OTHER WINDOW: WORLDS THROUGH THE TUNNEL

A Short Story by Shane Tovar

I drove my truck on the highway on a cloudy, stormy night for an emergency to see my mom in a hospital, to say goodbye to her for the last time. Her health hadn't done too well the past couple of years; now it was serious. She wouldn't make it.

I was going to see her one last time to let her move on. My brother and sister would be there too. I don't know why my brother was going to be there because I was the one that took care of Mom more than he did. Me and my brother had a big fight about sending Mom to a nursing home, but I put my foot down and said no. Do you know what else? He wanted to sell our father's house that all three of us built together for the family and for the next generation. The house was down in the countryside near our farm. It had been ten years since our big fight, so hopefully my brother and I could get over our differences and forget the past.

It was raining so much that I couldn't see a single thing; even the windshield washers weren't enough to see the road ahead. Then suddenly, my phone rang. It could be the hospital calling me about my mom's condition, so I answered the call and put it on speaker, and it was my brother calling me. "Jacob, where are you?" he said.

"Oh, hey, Joseph," I said, "my little brother. How you been?"

"What *little*? Who you calling little? You just nevermind. I'm already here at the hospital with Mom, and the doctor said she doesn't have long to live, so get here soon," Joseph said.

"All right, I'm trying to find a way to get there faster. See you there, bye." Then I hung up the phone and put on the map app to find a faster way to the hospital.

The map app found a shortcut through a tunnel just up ahead five minutes away. Five minutes later, I made it to the tunnel in a large mountain. It was amazing and strange to behold, and do you know what else was strange? That there were no cars or eighteen-wheelers driving through there.

I was hesitant to drive in, but I needed to go see my mom for one last time, so I drove into the tunnel. It was so dark I had to put on my high beams on front and top lights to see in the cold-hearted darkness.

Bravely, I kept on driving through the tunnel for two hours, and the hospital in the city was about five hours away. Now there were three hours left.

It was getting kind of boring, so I turned on the radio to boost up the mood, but I was barely getting any music, must have been because of the mountain blocking the signal.

At last there was a talk show, so I left the dial on the talk show. They talked about what funny stuff happened to people, and sports, and no politics, so I could relax.

It was weird that there was no one driving through the tunnel, no cars, no pickup trucks, or eighteen-wheelers to be seen, just me in my truck all alone in the dark.

Well, at least I had the radio on to keep me company, but the strangest thing happened. The radio started to act funny. The radio, it kept on skipping through the channels really fast with words that didn't make sense. One minute later, the radio started to talk to me. "Hel-lo, Jacob, w-e'v-e be-en wait-ing for you."

I didn't understand what was going on, but that wasn't normal to hear the radio talking to you.

Meanwhile, the truck started to shake, and everything got fuzzy, and I felt nothing, and I said, "What the hell is going on here?" Then seconds later, I suddenly crashed into a strange-looking tree that looked different from anything on Earth. How could that be?

I don't know how long I was out, maybe an hour or so, but while I was out, it sounded like loud noises, loud stomping and roaring, but how? Then I woke up and looked around me. It was dark and foggy. A cave right behind me was tall and narrow. In front of me was a tree or a large boulder or something, and it started to move on its own.

I thought it was a big mouth at first, but it was a giant leg of a monster. It was 500 feet tall and had a long neck and big teeth. The beast looked around then looked down upon its feet. I ran as fast as I could back to my wrecked truck and hid inside. The monster moved its neck down towards my truck and looked at it and smelled it.

I was too scared to get out of my truck, but I knew that I needed to survive, so I waited for the right moment to get out of the vehicle.

It smelled the truck again and opened its mouth to try to eat it whole. Now was my chance to make my escape. I opened the door to jump out while the truck was almost in its mouth.

Now that I was out of the truck, I ran behind a boulder to hide from the beast. Hopefully, I didn't get seen. Luckily, instead, it still had a hold on my truck with its mouth. The monster moved the truck left to right, then it ate the vehicle whole. I couldn't believe my eyes. My truck was gone forever. R.I.P., old friend. Then the truck exploded in its mouth while the beast continued to eat it.

But then it spit it out of its mouth, must be because it was metal and not meat. After the monster spit the truck out, it lifted its neck back up and started to walk away while I was still behind the boulder, fearing for my life. The long-necked monster walked away slowly with loud stomping and making the planet shake with all its weight.

A few minutes later, it was all clear, so I walked to see what was left of my truck, and it was all crushed like a pancake. All my stuff was gone because I had a large combat knife and my long 357 revolver, but the sun came out and shone on something metal. I walked over to where the sunshine was shining, and it was my favorite revolver with all six 357 Magnum rounds left. I couldn't believe it; I guess it fell out after the truck exploded.

Luckily, I had something to defend myself. After I found my revolver, I looked around for my other stuff. An hour later, I found my combat knife. It was in a big pile of poo. The poo was blue for some reason, but I didn't care, so I reached for my knife, and suddenly a giant worm came out and tried to eat me.

It opened its mouth, and it had a lot of teeth. Then the worm charged at me, trying to bite me, but I dodged it again and again, still trying to reach the combat knife. The monster worm charged with a final blow. Finally, I felt something hard—my knife! I didn't waste time. I got the knife out then held it with both hands and cut the monster worm's head off with a single swing down on its neck.

I fell backwards to the ground, all tired, and I couldn't get up, but I needed to keep on moving, or more of those worms would come.

First thing I needed was a bath because my body stank real bad, so I looked for a waterfall or just a lot of water, but I wondered if the water would be the same as the water on Earth. I would see.

Well, ten minutes later, I found a waterfall, and it was just like the water from Earth. Not sure it tasted the same, but first a bath before drinking the water.

After taking a bath, I found my backpack near the waterfall on a tree branch, and it wasn't too hard to climb, so now I was all set for survival, and I didn't have to carry that much.

I walked into the unknown and tried to see if there was any human on this planet at all, or other things like aliens just like any sci-fi movie or storybook, or if there was nothing here at all, just me. So I walked, walked, and walked until it was getting dark. Now I had better get some wood and sticks to make myself a campfire for the night.

While I was gathering the wood, I noticed something off, that there were four moons that were close to the planet. One was very close, and the second one was right behind the first one, and the last two were small. But you could still see them right beside the second moon.

In this very strange universe throughout the day there was a sun, no, two suns to be exact. How was that even possible? But at least I could breathe, and there was life on this planet, so everything was alright for now, hopefully.

* * *

My campfire was ready, and it was time to eat some MRE, but I only had one to spare, so I needed to eat just a little, bit by bit. That didn't mean I could only survive with just MRE. I could go hunt down my own food to survive this weird, unknown world.

I tried to go to sleep. I could hear strange, unusual sounds throughout the lonely, dark night, some small and some big sounds like a bomb went off. Hopefully, I wouldn't get eaten during the night. Moments later, I got used to the loud sounds and finally went to sleep, waiting for dusk to come.

Dusk was rising, and I got up, and still, strange alien sounds could be heard from afar, but that didn't scare me. I really didn't want to keep eating MREs. I needed some real food in my belly. But I didn't know what to expect from this world. All I knew was I couldn't be afraid. I needed to move and try to find a way back home to see my family and my mom. I must see her for the last time.

So I found a bent tree branch and used my combat knife to make a bow and arrow, and after that, I made a spear to stab or throw at whatever was charging me. I also set traps all around my camp and in the forest, so I was ready for food to come to me, but first I wanted to go on a hunt. So I walked into the unknown.

About these trees, they were almost like the trees back home, but most of them glowed in the dark, and some were on fire. Weird, right?

When I walked to find food, I saw some kind of fruit on one of the trees. It looked very good to eat. It had a yellow color to it and had a glow to it. It might have been poisonous, so I needed to be careful, but I was really hungry now, so I couldn't resist. I climbed up the strange tree and tried to reach the yellow fruit. Suddenly, the tree moved on its own.

Freaking out, I said, "Hey, what the hell?" Then I jumped off the tree and hit the ground while doing a belly roll. Then I looked back, and the tree started to transform into something so terrifying that no one could imagine. In the middle, it split into two parts with a lot of teeth on all sides, and it sprouted a lot of long, sharp vines.

Shooting an arrow at it for sure wouldn't work, but the tree monster had to have a weak spot somewhere. I just needed to find it.

Next, the tree monster started to attack with its sharp vines while roaring at me, so I used quick reflexes and my spear to cut the vines. I cut and dodged again. Then it cut my leg while I fell to the ground.

I yelled in pain and held my leg. The beast grabbed hold of me and carried me up high to its mouth. So, it would eat me. This was the end of me.

Then with faith and hope, I saw its eye inside the middle of its mouth. That must be its weak spot, but I didn't have my spear with me because I dropped it while the monster grabbed hold of my body. All I had was my combat knife on my right side. I tried to break free with my right arm to grab my knife. Then I threw my knife at its big eye, and it worked. It screamed in pain while letting me go.

When back on the ground, I grabbed my spear to finish the job while charging at it and jumping towards its eye and stabbing it. Then it made a final roar, and it died.

With relief, I dropped to the ground, just glad I didn't get eaten alive. But now, after that fight, I was really hungry. I needed to find food, but where? I didn't have time to sit, so I got up and grabbed my knife and my bow and arrow and my spear, and headed off to find something to eat.

Walking and still hungry for so long wasn't easy for a normal person. Good thing I was in the special forces for a long time. In another ten years, I would have been promoted to general.

Sadly, I quit after a failed mission that led almost all of my men to their deaths. At first, I never forgave myself after all that mess, but after some therapy, I forgave and forgot. I was moving on with my life.

Still walking in the wilderness and into the unknown, I heard something in the bushes. It moved all through the bushes. What came out was a strange, small alien creature with three long eyes and a fat body and hair, but it could be edible. The three-eyed, small alien didn't notice me, so I didn't waste time. I stabbed it straight through its body and put it in my leave bag I had made. Then more came out. I stabbed them for extra. Now I had something to eat.

Besides eating, I had more important stuff to take care of like my father's farm and hopefully getting along with my brother and sister and seeing my mom for the last time. I knew it might take a while, but I had faith.

TEXAS DRAWL

A Memoir Essay by Roma Johnson Holley

I grew up in the country just south of Sweetwater. I grew up a dirt-stained, sunburnt, scraped-up and tough-as-nails Farm Kid. I grew up working hard for everything we had. If we wanted to eat, we had to first feed it. Cows, chickens, pigs, you name it. If we wanted to harvest from our garden, we had to sow and hoe ... tomatoes, peppers, cucumbers, watermelons, okra, squash and cantaloupe, a bounty of delicious vegetables. We picked from rows and rows of black-eyed peas and green beans which my mama then canned. Even now the sight of Ball canning jars and lids bring back memories of summer. One of my favorite things my mama canned was chowchow. This tangy relish was made toward the end of the summer with green tomatoes, onions, and green and red peppers. I loved the spiciness the vinegar in this relish brought to any meal. We always had plenty to eat even in the winter and even in the years when our crops failed. Our pantry always had food while our cool cellar stored the root vegetables. I'm serious when I say I'm from the country.

Growing up in the country, I had a pretty strong drawl. It just came naturally. And it was not just because of the hard work and the food—although that was some good eating—but because of how I was raised. My folks were farmers and true country folks. When I was very young we grew cotton. I remember the brown-skinned migrant workers who came through to hoe the cotton, keeping the weeds from taking over, and then later, another group came through to pick it. They pulled long bags behind them, stuffing them full as they worked.

Mama would send me to the ends of the rows to meet the workers with a big jug of water. I couldn't understand a word being said—they spoke extremely fast and laughed a lot, and I'm sure they were chuckling at the little white country girl dragging a jug of water—but I did understand their gratitude for the refreshing water. A cold drink in that dry west Texas heat said more than words.

In later years, Daddy borrowed a cotton stripper from a neighbor. I thought we had hit the big time. We didn't have to hire anyone to harvest anymore. I can remember being in the trailer behind the cotton stripper that was shooting out the cotton being stripped from the stalks. My brother and I were "trouncing" the cotton, packing it down so we could get more in the trailer. At first we thought it was great fun, but it did not take long for us to be covered in cotton. It stuck to our sweat and infiltrated every pore of our body. So much for having fun. I just wanted to take a breath that wasn't filled with cotton. At the end of the day, we were so worn out and sore, we barely had the energy to eat supper and fall into bed. Trouncing was work, but work is what we did!

(I can remember hearing my cousins tell stories about trouncing the cotton and the stripper shooting out a rattlesnake. Thank goodness that never happened to me—I have a strong dislike of any kind of snake, dead or alive.)

After a few years, Daddy rotated crops to growing wheat. My brother and I plowed up the rows of cotton stalks, and Daddy planted wheat. I thought, surely this will be easier than cotton. Well, not so much. Wheat chaff is just as bad if not worse than cotton. Just being around the wheat while it was being harvested was like walking through a fog. Chaff stuck to our clothes and got into our socks and shoes. Even when we were able to stop for a few minutes, the wind swirled the chaff around us, and it got into our water and on our food if we had brought lunch. Again, it was demanding work, but it was necessary.

In our youth we played king-of-the-mountain on hay bales and played hide-and-seek among the stacks. As we got older, my brother and I had to haul the hay. At first I got to drive the truck pulling the trailer. I had to sit on a large cushion in order to see over the steering wheel, but my long legs had no problem reaching the foot pedals. I could only drive in "granny gear," but to a ten-year-old, it felt like freedom. As I got bigger and stronger, Daddy had me walking the field, throwing hay bales onto the trailer so my brother could stack them. The only ride I got was back to the barn where we unloaded and stacked the bales. And again, more snake stories. Rattlesnakes baled up in the hay or hiding under a stack. Just thinking about it makes me shiver.

Yep, we were country kids through and through. Our Texas drawl was just part of us. We didn't even realize we had one.

When I was twelve, Daddy developed health issues and had to stop farming. Mama, who had been a licensed vocational nurse before we were born, got a job at a nursing home in Bronte, about thirty miles south of the farm. She drove back and forth for about a year. But because she worked the evening shift and got off work after 11 p.m., it could be a dangerous drive home. So, my parents decided to move there. Even though we only moved thirty miles, it felt like another world. We were like the Beverly Hillbillies—except instead of moving to California, we moved from a farm to a huge town of 939 people. At school we went from having four kids in our class to having twenty-four. We rode our bicycles to school which was a huge change from having to ride a school bus. Culture shock doesn't even begin to describe what was happening to us. It really felt weird. There were times when I really missed the quiet life of the farm. I wasn't used to so many people and so many cars. It was only later in life that I realized what a great opportunity this was for my family.

But we still worked. Mama hired me out to mow the yards of elderly neighbors. I raked leaves and pulled weeds, too. All of that work on the farm had prepared me well. Also, Daddy hired me and my brother out to haul hay. I can't tell you how many long, hot, summer days were spent walking the fields of our neighbors. How many times we fell into bed at night exhausted. But we learned the value of hard work. We learned to appreciate the fact that our hard work helped feed the world. The summer after I graduated high school, Daddy even hired me out to plow fields before college started. This turned out to be a blessing in disguise as not only did it help the elderly gentleman who owned the property, but it also helped me with funds for college.

After graduating high school, I attended Abilene Christian University for a year. It was there that I started realizing just how country I was. My fellow students might not have known my name, but they knew my voice and my drawl. They *knew* I was from the country. After a year of struggling to find my way, I decided college wasn't for me. The next fall, I went through a program in Lubbock called A.I.M., Adventures In Missions. It was a missionary apprentice program hosted by Sunset Church of Christ. I attended six months of intense Bible training and learning to share the gospel, and then I went to Scotland for eighteen months. Let's talk about a drawl. I thought by going to Scotland I wouldn't have to learn a foreign language. Right?!! The first night I was riding a two-decker bus in Edinburgh and there were two elderly Scottish ladies sitting across from me just a "blethering" away. I couldn't understand them, and they couldn't understand me. It was very comical and just a little scary. My time spent in Scotland and traveling Europe not only enriched my life, but it also made me lose a little bit of my drawl. Oh, you could still tell I was from Texas, but I was definitely influenced by all of the other languages that I was exposed to.

Fast forward to me returning to the States, marrying a California boy in the military and being transferred to the Philippines. My Texas drawl was still there, but it was getting watered down, a consequence of so many different experiences.

When we left the Philippines, we were stationed in California at Edwards Air Force Base. While there, we liked to travel, and so there was a time when we drove up to Utah. We spent several days there and by the time we were ready to leave, I was beyond tired. We finally headed home and stopped at a grocery store to get a bag of ice. I went into the store and couldn't find the ice box. I asked a clerk where the ice box was. She looked at me like I had three heads. She said, "Excuse me?" I asked again, "Where is your ice box?" Again, she looked at me like I was speaking a foreign language. "Where do you keep your bags of ice?" I said very slowly. "Ice. I-C-E." She said, "Oh, ice. I'm so sorry, I thought you were asking me where the a$$ box was." (What is an a$$ box??) I just wanted to say, "Seriously?" But I just didn't have the energy. I just shook my head and bought my ice.

The point is that when I was really tired, I would slip back into the country drawl that I grew up with. This drawl is as much a part of me as the cotton that invaded my young body and the wheat chaff that we inhaled. This drawl is as much a part of me as the sweat poured into the hale bales we stacked and the tractors we drove. This drawl comes from growing up and working hard in the country. We didn't know any better. That's just who we were and what we did. It's still a part of me. I like to think I earned this drawl.

So, that's my story. I'll never forget that clerk from Utah looking for an a$$ box. And I'll never forget the black dirt that my drawl came from. That drawl is as deep rooted as a pecan tree. And I love pecans! But that's another story.

FIRST RESPONDER

Jim Wilson

You called crying so I came
and met you in the library garden.
We walked toward each other
and fist bumped a greeting.

Yet our fingers quickly intertwined
as we walked side by side
down the winding flagstone path
lined with yellow pansies.

Even in the morning sun and open air
we knew it was beautifully unsafe.
I coughed softly into my elbow
as per Center for Disease Control guidelines.

We talked quietly and supportively.
You said you had a low-grade fever,
and your test results would be back
Saturday but we needed each other today.

Times were so uncertain. An hour later
back at the cars we virtually hugged.
Trading mask-less full smiles inches away
we went back to our semi-seclusion.

Three days later I tested positive.
You were already in the hospital.
In two weeks, I had tested negative three times
and felt well enough to attend your funeral.

At graveside, our social distancing could be no greater
as I dropped a face mask and pair of blue latex gloves
down on your coffin for you to use in the next world
in case it was no more just than this one.

DON'T SHOOT, I'M A MADDLE *OR* THE BALLAD OF BIMBO

A Mostly True Memoir Essay by Jennifer Neville Maddle

My father-in-law, James Cordell Maddle Senior was a bigger-than-life caricature of a man, at least in his later years when I knew him. Tall and robust with a booming voice to match, he loomed large over his family as the undisputed patriarch of the whole Maddle Clan. Denim overalls and loafers were his preferred daily attire, except for the occasional wedding or funeral, in which case he opted for dark slacks with a belt *and suspenders*, not being one to take unnecessary chances at that stage of his life. Apparently this was not always the case, however.

James Maddle Senior was a born storyteller. It didn't take me long to become wise to his turn of phrase when he got going on something that he thought he could get away with telling, but I've always loved hearing other people's stories almost as much as I've loved telling my own. We were both shameless embellishers. I think that's one of the things we enjoyed the most about each other. Kindred spirits, in a weird sort of way. I was already pretty fond of him, he having been instrumental in producing the man that I would marry, James Cordell Maddle *Junior,* a vivid storyteller in his own right, but he absolutely sealed the deal the day that he passed on this recycled memory to me as I sat enraptured on the edge of my seat and he wove his tale.

* * *

Early in his second marriage to a woman named Faye, James Maddle had made the decision to take his new bride on a trip to the Great Smoky Mountains. His kids were all grown by this time, and it would be one of *their* first trips alone together. James had been born and raised in Tennessee in the foothills of the Smokies near a town called Monterey. He loved to tell stories of his time living in the mountains in his childhood, when he and his own father hunted for black bear to keep food on the table. Back then he was known as Cordell by his family and friends, mostly because James was a family name, and it got pretty hard to tell them all apart when they got in the same room together, I would imagine. Cordell Maddle, I have no doubt, was as memorable a character then as he was when he told me this story decades later.

It seems that when James Cordell fudged the date on a birth certificate to get himself enlisted in the U.S. Army and away from the Great Smokies and the only life he'd ever known, he grabbed onto the opportunity and never looked back. Once in the military, he was not only able to escape a life of working in the coal mines, homebrewing moonshine, and dodging the damn revenuers, he was also earning a steady paycheck to send home to his family. The cost, however, was leaving Monterey and the mountains for a number of years, as fate would have it. He would later meet and marry Goldie Cox Maddle and embark on growing his own branch of the Maddle Family tree right here in Texas. And although he had come from extremely humble beginnings fraught with questionable choices and doing what you had to do to survive a life of poverty in the mountains, James Cordell Maddle Senior had actually ended up doing quite well for himself, post military. So by the time he was on that trip back to the Smokies for the first time in a very long time, he was driving a brand new giant luxury Cadillac, roughly the size of a yacht, with a new wife in tow, and living life large.

Perhaps arriving back in his old stomping grounds unannounced and in such a showy manner after being gone for so many years wasn't something he had thought through all the way. Or maybe it was. Who's to say? As the story was told to me, James wasn't really certain if there were still any Maddles squatting on the old homestead, as most of his siblings had by this time married and moved on themselves. And because it had been a number of years since he had been in the area, he wasn't absolutely certain that the winding mountain road he was currently traversing en route to what he hoped was his old childhood home was even the right one. And because he didn't want to appear unsure of himself in front of Faye, and winding mountain roads are notoriously difficult to navigate backwards, he refused to turn around and just plowed on until he was, in fact, absolutely certain that he had taken a wrong turn somewhere. It was approaching nightfall by this time, and he knew better than to be out and about in the mountains in that big ol' Caddy after dark, lest *he* be mistaken for a revenuer and not at all welcomed by the mountain folk who still, no doubt, ran their own homemade distilleries and brewed their own homemade moonshine, by the light of the actual moon, way back in the mountains, which was where James and Faye were now currently headed. And just as he was about to throw in the towel and confess to Faye that he was sure they were lost and that it was going to be imperative that he find a way to turn the car around as soon as possible and get them down out of the mountains before it got any darker, two men, one from either side of the road, both holding ominously large rifles, stepped out in front of the Caddy, prohibiting them from traveling any farther.

At this point James was forced to pull the car to a halt in the middle of the winding mountain road and had no choice but to exit the vehicle in a cautious manner, hands held aloft, his parting words to Faye, "Stay in the car ... but run if you have to."

As he departed the smoothly idling luxury Cadillac and stood to reach his full, well-over-six-foot, overall-clad height, he offered only these words in that distinctive booming voice of his: "Don't shoot! I'm a Maddle!"

And with that, the two men with guns drawn, craned their own overall-clad selves forward and squinted their eyes to get a better look.

"Cordell? ... Is that you?" came the response from the one who seemed to be in charge as he quickly lowered his weapon, and just like that, as if no time had passed at all, it was a Maddle family reunion, complete with moonshine and plenty of black bear for everyone.

* * *

It would be many, many years later that I would share that story with my sister-in-law Sandy as we reminisced about her dad and old family stories. She laughed and told me she was sure that was probably one of her dad's made up stories, as she had never heard it before in her life. I've always understood that you can't bullshit a bullshitter, but that must not always be true, because I fell for that one hook, line, and sinker.

Over the years, I enjoyed remembering that story of Monterey, Tennessee, told to me by my father-in-law, true or maybe *not* so true, and the remaining Maddle population who no doubt still lived there, somewhere in the foothills of the Smokies. Knowing that James Maddle had been a name passed down through generations, and being married to the current James Maddle, I was curious to see if there might be evidence of anyone by that name still residing in the area. A quick Google search indicated that there was, indeed, a James *Albert* Maddle living in Monterey, Tennessee, apparently something of a well-known local character, who went by the name of Bimbo. Bimbo Maddle. Who turned out to be, we would later discover, a very distant cousin.

I first encountered the stories of ol' Bimbo through the op-ed section of the local hometown newspaper in Monterey, via internet, of course. There were several editorials concerning Bimbo Maddle. It seems that our distant cousin was actually something of a minor celebrity, in his neck of the woods at least. I learned that Bimbo was homeless. By choice. Despite the fact that he had family in town, who by all accounts would have offered him a helping hand had he chosen to accept it, Bimbo apparently preferred the excitement and the freedom of living on the streets and going wherever the wind blew him. He was known to be in constant motion, walking in his tattered and well-loved shoes wherever he went, a true lover of nature. The editorials came in the form of letters of concern for Bimbo as the weather vacillated between the extremes of cold winters and warm summers in the foothills of the Great Smoky Mountains. Many residents seemed to worry that Bimbo, their token unhoused resident, would sooner or later succumb to its ravages, so much so that there was a collection taken up at one point to get Bimbo into some shelter. A small apartment was procured in his name, modestly furnished, and stocked with nourishing food and drink. But when a well-meaning resident came by a few days later to check in, Bimbo was nowhere to be found. There was, in fact, no evidence to be seen that Bimbo had spent a night there at all. When he was finally located at the edge of town, resting his head under the shade of a large tree, and questioned, he merely suggested that they should probably "give that nice place to someone who really needs it."

The concern for Bimbo continued, but his will remained steadfast. Some years later he apparently came into a few thousand dollars on his own from winnings on a lottery ticket. The town thought, "Now Bimbo will put that money to use and take care of himself," or at least that's what the article in the newspaper said. I had taken it upon myself to keep up with the Bimbo-related goings on in Monterey and was happy to see that he had been the recipient of such an unexpected windfall. But when I checked back in a few months later, there was ol' Bimbo on the front page of the paper, grinning ear to ear, holding one of those giant oversized checks. He had donated that money to the local library, further establishing himself as Monterey's own homeless hometown hero.

Not much was printed about Bimbo after that, or if there was, I didn't find it. In all honesty, I kind of got out of the habit of checking in on Bimbo regularly. The next time it occurred to me to look him up, I found only his obituary. By all accounts, the concerned residents of

Monterey had been correct in their assumptions that he would eventually succumb to the elements. It seemed as if he finally did. He was buried in the local cemetery at the edge of town, surrounded by the very trees under which he had so often rested his head, or so I imagined. The photo of his grave marker that I was able to find online was adorned with what I assumed were amateur freehand drawings of a well-worn pair of shoes and a section of shade trees, two of the things that he appeared to love the most, now presiding over his soul for all eternity. I always said that if I ever made it to Monterey, Tennessee, I would stop in to pay my respects to our cousin Bimbo, character that he was.

And eventually, it happened, as way leads 'round to way, that I did finally find myself in Monterey, Tennessee, on vacation with my husband, the current reigning James Maddle. We made our way to that sad little cemetery surrounded by all the trees, and looked, and looked for Bimbo, our cousin. His marker, it seemed, was nowhere to be found. The cemetery was quite old, and not at all well cared for. There was no registry of graves, no number to call, just a lot of overgrown grass, rendering those beneath it virtually incognito. We left Monterey a little sad that day. I had really wanted to find ol' Bimbo and maybe leave him a flower or something. It seemed that we had failed him somehow. I wondered if anybody had ever taken the time to visit him, in death, if not in life. I never got to meet cousin Bimbo, but if I know one thing about the line of James Maddles that he descends from, there is one hell of a family reunion in Heaven every time one of them walks through those pearly gates, complete with moonshine and plenty of black bear for everyone.

FIX YOUR FACE

A Short Story by Priscilla Bettis

Henrietta Armstrong sat her worn-out self in the old wicker chair on the porch. She squinted against the late afternoon sun and inhaled. The air smelled like the wild bergamot that clutched the rusty mailbox post, the Snews' maturing wheat, and the remaining sweet tea in the souvenir glass sitting on the windowsill.

Her sister had bought the glass years ago. A painted image of a Ferris wheel and the words *Coffee County Fair* decorated the side of the glass. The paint was flaking, but Henrietta hated Ferris wheels anyway.

She yawned. In the gutter of the porch roof, one of those pesky swallows scratched, chirped, then finally settled into silence as if it knew she needed the rest. She'd let blind Scully in his rattly mail truck wake her up.

Scully ought not to be driving at all. A dent marked the side of the mailbox where he hit it the first time. The second time he hit it, he left it cattywampus. Without leaving her seat, Henrietta appraised the mailbox at the edge of the road. It was a mite funny looking, but the stubborn thing was still standing, so there was no use in replacing it.

Scully should be bringing the new *Ladies' Home Journal* this week. Word had it that in this issue Angie Dickinson spilled the beans on JFK.

Closing her eyes, she yawned again. No nearby neighbors to pester her, no husband to pick up after, no siblings to—

"Mama, I'm hungry!"

The girl. For a moment, Henrietta had forgotten she no longer lived in the historic family farmhouse by herself. She pried her eyes open.

"I'm on the porch," Henrietta called through the window screen. "And I'm not your mother."

Her niece's footsteps clonked from inside the house, growing louder until the door opened and out tumbled Lacey.

"Your dress is dirty," Henrietta said. She sat forward. "Is that *my* dress?"

The dimwitted girl spun, and the full-skirted shirtwaist dress flared like a flower blooming. "I found it in the trunk in the yellow room."

The yellow bedroom, Henrietta's room when she was young, when the dress fit her. Or almost fit her. Lacey filled it out better across the bust.

"What'd you spill on it?" Henrietta asked.

"Ketchup."

The girl had spilt something on herself almost every day of the two months she'd been living with Henrietta. Seemed like a low IQ came with clumsiness.

"It's still pretty, Mama. Can I keep it?"

Henrietta hauled herself out of the chair. "Yes, and any other clothes in that trunk that fit you." It'd save Henrietta money not having to purchase clothes for the unexpected boarder.

Lacey was going to eat her out of house and home if Henrietta didn't marry her off. And right quick.

Lacey spun again. "It's like buyin' a new dress!"

"Don't drop your g's. Show a little class." Class would attract the marrying sort of man. Henrietta shooed Lacey inside and followed after her. "Soak that dress in the utility sink in cold water with a little vinegar. Directly now, before the stain sets."

"Yes, Mama."

"And I'm not your—"

Lacey had already disappeared down the hallway.

If Marla, Henrietta's sister, hadn't got the cancer, if Marla's no-good husband hadn't run off in the first place just as soon as he realized his baby girl's windmill was missing a few blades, Henrietta wouldn't be stuck with the child.

Henrietta took inventory of the items in the icebox. They'd have to go to the grocery store.

Lacey came into the kitchen wearing another dress Henrietta hadn't seen in years. Its green calico set the girl's brown eyes to glowing, but there was something askew about the bodice.

Henrietta leaned in, scrutinizing the placket. "You missed a button. Go fix your face, and we'll shop for supper."

A perfectly shaped lower lip slipped forward in a pout. "George says there ain't nothin'—*notheeng*—broken about my face."

Henrietta rolled her eyes. The young handyman was proving a source of trouble when it came to Lacey, but he charged half of what anyone else would, so she couldn't get rid of him.

Through the open windows came a hollow whistle from the pipe factory in town. It was quitting time. All the young men wanted to work at the factory, seeing how they paid more than the $2.10 minimum wage, but apparently you needed an *in* from a town councilman to get a job there.

"And Mizz New—"

"Mrs. Snew." Henrietta corrected her niece.

"—says my beauty don't come from the outside but comes from God's beautiful Spirit inside, and if folks could just take a peek in there, they'd see all the pretty I have."

Those Bible-thumping Snews ought to keep to themselves. "I told you to fix your face."

With her hands on her hips, Lacey stomped out of the kitchen.

Henrietta grabbed her purse and car keys then stepped outside on the porch to cool off in the breeze while she waited for Lacey.

George rode up on his bicycle with the missing front fender.

"You already went home for the day," Henrietta said to the high school dropout her sister had recommended before she died.

He's had it tough, Marla had said. *He just needs a break.*

"No, ma'am," George replied. After lowering the kickstand, he wiped sweat off his face and neck with the bandanna he kept in his back pocket. "I said I'd be back after I took care of some business with Doc. I need to hurry and get those repairs done on the storm shelter."

Henrietta cocked her head. "Supposed to be clear all through the week. What's the hurry?"

"You see, ma'am, Doc was—"

Just then, Lacey emerged from the house. She was wearing too much rouge, but otherwise, she had done a good job with her makeup.

A smile jumped to George's face, and Henrietta attempted to move between the two young people. Both of them were too quick, though, and before Henrietta knew it, they stood on the porch with nary daylight between them.

Lacey didn't know any better about the two of them getting involved, but George should. He lived above old Doc's single-car garage. Henrietta, being George's employer, knew exactly how much he made, which was hardly enough to keep air in his bicycle tires. It was only supposed to be a temporary job. *'Til something else comes along,* he kept saying. But it'd been over a year since Henrietta hired him, and he hadn't found anything better. If the two young folk got hitched, they wouldn't fit into Doc's puny garage apartment. They'd both end up under Henrietta's roof.

And Henrietta couldn't have that.

Why, oh *why* did Marla make Henrietta promise not to put Lacey in an institution?

George took off his ball cap and smoothed his hair. "You're looking mighty pretty, Lacey. New dress?"

What did he think he was doing, some kind of old-fashioned courting ritual?

Lacey stepped back then twirled once, the green calico rising and flashing her legs.

"I haven't seen you at church in a while," he said with his eyes looking like they wished for another twirl.

"My other mama died."

Henrietta cursed at the sky then snapped at Lacey. "Get inside and fix your ... your hair."

Lacey tugged on a lock. "There ain't noth*eeng* wrong with my hair. Besides, I just wanted to ask George about Doc."

"Inside, Lacey. Directly!" Henrietta gripped her car keys so hard the flesh of her fingers screamed with pain.

After Lacey had gone inside, Henrietta pointed a key like a jagged finger in George's direction. "The girl is not for you."

He put his cap back on. "She's old enough to make up her own mind."

"She's special."

"Sure is." He grinned.

Folding her arms, Henrietta said, "That's not what I meant. She's aiming to get herself a man, and I need you to get out of her way."

George's smile dropped. "You mean you're aiming to get rid of her. You needn't be in such a hurry. Any man would be pleased to have Lacey on his arm."

"Now wait a minute." She scowled. "I've seen the way you look at her. It wouldn't be right to take advantage of a girl like Lacey. She's only got one thing going for her. If she didn't have her looks, you wouldn't give her a second thought."

His nostrils flared, and he stepped closer. "This is the way it is, Miss Armstrong. First, I'm a God-fearing gentleman and would never take advantage of a woman. Second, she's got more going for her than all the women in town combined."

Henrietta chuckled. "The girl—"

"She bakes a mean blackberry pie." He raised one finger.

"She does?"

"She's the only woman who can calm the Millers' cranky baby in the church nursery." He raised another finger. "She's a better gardener than you, or have you noticed her beans and turnips popping up out back?" Another finger.

"How dare you." Henrietta's words emerged from between clenched teeth.

"She's got Psalm 23, the first chapter of John, and all of Jude memorized."

He was wrong. He had to be all wrong. Henrietta swallowed.

The screen door creaked open, and Lacey stepped out. "I'm ready," she said. She walked delicately down the porch steps and toward the Oldsmobile.

Henrietta hugged her purse to her chest and, giving George a wide margin, hurried after her niece.

Eyeing Lacey's movements, Henrietta realized the graceful walking tips she'd been giving Lacey were paying off, and Henrietta purposely blocked George's view of Lacey's womanly stride.

"You're fired," Henrietta said over her shoulder. Hopefully, there'd be an eligible bachelor wandering the aisles of the grocery store.

Pings of rocks on metal announced the arrival of blind Scully and his mail truck. He sped past the mailbox in a plume of red dust. Henrietta huffed. Scully didn't deliver her new *Ladies' Home Journal* after all. There was only one more house, the Snews' place, and then he'd come clattering back. Best not to start the Olds until he was out of the way.

Lacey broke into a run. "Mail's here."

Oh, for crying out loud. Henrietta watched the girl, too tired to run after her. She sighed, and then she yelled, "No, girl, Scully didn't bring us anything. Now, get in the car."

But Lacey was too far down the drive.

Scully's truck was rattling its way back, throwing dust and noise into the air.

Lacey yanked open the mailbox. She crouched and peered inside.

"Lacey!" George's voice thundered. He sprinted past Henrietta. "The mail truck, watch out!"

Lacey stood to her full height and looked toward Scully's truck. His side-view mirror was the same height as her head.

George's legs pumped.

Henrietta screamed.

Lacey jerked away, but not far enough. The sound of the mirror striking her face was like the sound of a ripe tomato hitting the kitchen floor. She collapsed.

Blind Scully and his mail truck continued on their way while Lacey's blood quenched the thirsty dust of the road.

George knelt beside her and placed his hand on her shoulder.

Lacey twitched.

"She's alive!" He scooped her up and carried her to the Oldsmobile. "Open the back door. We have to take her to the hospital."

Henrietta stood motionless, gawping at Lacey's once-beautiful face. Her cheek was slashed open, exposing teeth. Her eye was already swelling shut. The whole mess would leave terrible scars.

"The door, Miss Armstrong." George's words came out in a growl and startled Henrietta into motion.

George eased Lacey into the car then settled in beside her and cradled her head. He pressed his bandanna against her cheek.

Recoiling at the sight of all that blood, Henrietta closed the back door then hastened herself behind the wheel. On the way to town, she kept glancing back at her passengers.

George's face was glowing with sweat and something else, too. "Does it hurt, Lacey?" His voice was tender.

"No, just when I talk." Her words were wet and slurred.

"So don't talk," he said.

"But I can't help it. I want to know if Doc came through for you."

What was the girl talking about? Henrietta reached the juncture at the highway that led into town. They turned right, leaving the dusty road behind.

"He did, Lacey," George said. "Just like he said he would."

They drove in silence for a moment save for the hiss of the air conditioner and Lacey's splattery breath.

"Ow," Lacey said.

"What?" George's voice sounded desperate. "What is it, darling?"

"It also hurts when I smile."

George chuckled. "So don't smile."

"I can't help it. I'm so happy."

Henrietta nearly ran off the road. The blow must have damaged the girl's brain, what little brain she had.

"It's like Mizz New said," Lacey continued. "My insides are showin', so now everyone can see how pretty I am. Even Mama."

George held her closer. "You're right, Lacey. You're even more pretty now. Even more."

Henrietta brushed aside their childish words. She couldn't help but think what a chore it was going to be to clean all that blood off the back seat.

WORKING OUT

An Anecdote by Ruth V. York

My tween-age son was offered a job helping install an above-ground pool.

"Good for you!" I congratulated him. "Piece of cake, huh?"

"I don't know," he said, hesitating. "They asked another kid to do it, but he didn't work out."

"So?" I asked.

Doubt warred with honesty as he explained the obvious. "Mom, neither do I!"

THE FEED SACK TOTE

A Memoir Essay by Rob Witherspoon

The sign out front of the Sinclair station advertised Regular for thirty-six cents a gallon, and for four cents more you could get a gallon of Ethyl; the Beatles broke up, the crew of Apollo 13 let NASA know, "Houston, we have a problem." Oh, yeah, the Vietnam War was in full swing, where U.S. and South Vietnamese troops invaded Cambodia, and the National Guard killed four students at Kent State. There was a good deal of friction between young folks and old folks, but not so much in our little town. The younger generation rebelled some, such is their nature, but nothing radical like happened elsewhere.

We watched the evening news with body counts and maps with strange names and tried to keep track of where our friends and loved ones were stationed. We knew my cousin A.D. was in the Rice cemetery, killed by a VC sniper's bullet. Pictures of protests and demonstrations covered the newspapers. *Young people speaking their minds, getting so much resistance from behind*. Not so much in Bristol, Texas. Kids still said, "Yes, sir" and "No, sir." We said *ma'am* a lot and held the doors for girls and women. Merle Haggard's "Okie from Muskogee" was still popular. We didn't burn anything that didn't need burning, and the local constabulary made sure the only sit-ins were down at the Sinclair station where my father and other locals would congregate. In summer they sat on the bench outside and drank Co-cola and watched the June bugs. In winter they sat inside on cases of motor oil, drank coffee, and played dominoes.

It was at the Sinclair station, the only gas station in town, where one generation threw down the gauntlet to another. My cousin Tom, a strapping young man who attended SMU on a track scholarship, had gained a good bit of muscle as a result of the college weight room and a generous buffet provided to athletes. My father and Uncle James were former Marines who served during the Korean Conflict. Uncle Vernon, Tom's father, was a Marine veteran who made three island landings in the Pacific during WWII, got stabbed in hand-to-hand fighting, and received a Purple Heart. Vietnam killed one cousin and left another badly wounded, both Marines. Tom was in the Navy Reserve, which didn't cut much mustard with the older generation, especially combat vets.

One day, Tom drove by to fill up his car, appropriately enough a Ford Mustang. He parked and joined the men on the bench, an SMU tee shirt stretched tight across his chest, his biceps bulging like twelve-pound hams. He was the youngest of the bunch, except for me, and I didn't have any place in an adult conversation. Whenever someone joined the group, the men there welcomed the newcomer with a clever insult. It's too long ago to remember exactly what they said, but the gist of it was that he was a young whippersnapper and that all that weightlifting didn't amount to beans compared to doing *real* work. Harrumph! College boys.

That led to a clever rejoinder of which time has obscured the words, but it amounted to, *I can do anything you old farts can do, better, faster, farther, and longer.*

It was here that my father took up the challenge. My father was pushing forty, working hard as a carpenter and keeping up our small farm and ranch. He ate beans and cornbread and drank a quart of whole milk pretty nearly every day. He told Tom that he had come to town to get a hundred pounds of horse and mule feed and that he bet he could tote two fifty-pound sacks from the feed store to our house and that Tom could not. My cousin accepted the challenge but stipulated that he would hoist a barbell with one-hundred pounds of steel plates onto his shoulders and race my father. The conditions were acceptable and Tom drove to his parents' house to retrieve his barbell and weights. My father walked across the road to the feed store, made his purchase and set the feed sacks on the loading dock.

Tom returned and prepared his burden. The men from the Sinclair station served witness as he loaded the plates onto the barbell. They all attested that the load amounted to the agreed upon weight. There was a towel wrapped around the bar and secured in place with athletic tape. Tom wore sporting apparel and cinched a wide leather weightlifter's belt around his waist.

Tom cleaned, jerked and gently lowered the bar onto his shoulders. My father, dressed in jeans, a pearl-snap shirt and cowboy boots, bent to the feed sacks, wrapped his arms around them, and hoisted them onto his shoulders. He took a moment to balance them, and said, "Go."

It was seven-tenths of a mile from the feed store to our front porch, the negotiated finish line. The men strode off. The first two hundred yards were up a shallow hill that topped out and then leveled off for about a quarter mile and then dropped off sharply toward the Trinity River bottoms. Half of the race would be downhill, but the start would determine who could coast.

Tom and my father were both six foot-three, long legged and lean, so they were evenly matched in terms of stature. They went stride for stride up the hill, cowboy boots clicking the pavement and Tom's athletic shoes slapping asphalt.

They crested the hill, Tom ahead, but my father was not far behind. By now, sweat-stained tee shirt and pearl snap alike. Tom rolled his head and hunched his shoulders to move the bar to a different position and avoid chafing. My father stopped momentarily to adjust the balance of one of the sacks that had slipped a little too far forward and then trudged on. They were nearly across the level stretch and approaching the intersection where Slate Rock Road picks up and begins its descent. A slow procession of vehicles from the Sinclair station followed, honking and shouting encouragement. Everyone had bet on my father, even Uncle Vernon, Tom's dad.

The Farm to Market Road turned west but they continued straight, walking onto the blacktop road where county maintenance was sporadic and slap-dash. Even though they were going downhill, there were potholes and roadkill to negotiate. If the county commissioner had been more diligent, the race might have ended differently. Three hundred yards from the finish line, sweat pouring down his face and into his eyes, Tom didn't see the dinner plate sized void in the asphalt. He took a misstep, stumbled and the barbell slipped from his hands. It rolled into the bar ditch.

My father plodded along and stopped alongside Tom. He was in no better condition, soaked in sweat and breathing heavily. He had quit smoking three years before. "That's pretty far," he said, visually measuring the distance between the barbell and the finish line. He took another step. "This is farther."

My father, with the end in sight, strolled down the hill. But when he turned into our driveway, the recalcitrant feed sack slid from his shoulder and burst on the gravel. He slogged up the driveway and set the remaining sack on the porch.

I got a shovel and salvaged as much of the busted sack as I could. While I shoveled, Tom walked past. The barbell and weights were back on his shoulders, a grim look of determination on his face. If possible, he was taking even longer strides up the driveway.

He reached the porch and dropped the bar. "One hundred pounds," he said. "ALL the way."

My father grinned and extended his hand. "Let's call it a draw."

This is a mostly true story. Gaps in my 54-year memory are filled with plausible embellishments.

TEMPEST

Shann Tajiah

I do risky things now
Out of my mind
standing beneath the storming sky
surrounded by the crack of lightning
and the roll of thunder
soaking up every cold rain drop
feeling the sting of hail
all so I can feel
so I can hide my tears
and drown the screams
that shape your name.

THE TRAGIC TALE OF BYRON PARRISH

A Nonfiction Narrative by Helen Cozart

The history of West Texas is rich with tales of heroes and villains. Our story today, however, is decidedly not about a hero. It is about a villain—a liar, an abuser, a criminal, and a drunkard—whose life was a relentless cascade of self-inflicted chaos. His name was Byron Parrish.

A simple search for Byron Parrish might lead one to believe he was a decorated Texas Ranger. Yet even a slightly deeper dive into the records reveals this is false. Byron Parrish's story is far more complex and overwhelmingly negative. He was no hero, and it's no surprise that he ultimately died in jail.

The Myth and the Man

To understand the myth of Byron Parrish, Texas Ranger, we must first examine its primary architect: Boyce House. House, a renowned Texas author, created works ranging from accurate summations to outright tall Texas tales. In his later years, his reputation became that of a folklorist, and his stories grew in proportion to his popularity, often sacrificing accuracy for dramatic flair. Byron Parrish became famous because House reported on him favorably, making Parrish seem larger than life. Very little of what Boyce House claimed about Byron Parrish was true.

Born in Mason, Texas, in 1875, Parrish settled in Portales, New Mexico, early in his adult life. By 1902, he had a curious reputation as a "reformed drunkard" speaking on intemperance to church ladies—an image profoundly at odds with his later life. This supposed reformation didn't last, even though by 1907, he was a constable.

It was in 1907 that Parrish shot and killed Deputy Sheriff W.E.

Tipton. Parrish was a constable in Portales; Tipton a deputy in Curry County, working out of Texico—about 30 minutes apart. It seems unlikely they would ever know each other, but Tipton lived in Portales, commuting daily. Parrish, known for often stepping out of his jurisdiction, is the antagonist in this story. They'd had previous encounters where Tipton questioned Parrish's authority and requested he disarm or leave.

Parrish seemed to operate like a bounty hunter. In this instance, he tried to fill a warrant from Woods County, Oklahoma, by looking for a suspect in Texico. Again, Tipton confronted him about being armed outside his jurisdiction. This escalated to barroom fisticuffs, with each trying to take the other's weapon. The bartender even got involved, disarming Parrish. Then both officers tried to take Tipton's gun. Parrish was shot in the hand, and Tipton was shot in the eye, dying immediately.

Parrish was arrested and released on $10,000 bond. He was found not guilty by a jury a year later, and remarkably, continued to work in law enforcement during that entire time.

Oklahoma Fraud and False Claims

Whether or not he truly committed murder, by 1912, Parrish had left Portales for Oklahoma. He was hired as an enforcement officer in Guymon, Oklahoma, where in March, he made news for a massive cleanup of illegal booze and gambling. Here, a pattern emerged: Parrish created a gap in criminal activity by shutting down the illegal activities then exploited the gap by filling the void himself.

Fraud was also lucrative. One scandalous example occurred in Guymon in 1912. Court witnesses, including arresting officers, were paid for their time. In April, Parrish, who could have worked only ten days, fraudulently filed claims under various names, asserting he had worked 115 days. He received witness certificates worth over $100, cashing them before the fraud was discovered. He was ultimately charged with perjury. By 1913, he had left law enforcement for traveling piano sales.

The Myth of the Texas Ranger

Next, we encounter Governor James Ferguson, well known for his corruption. Boyce House's 1935 book, *Were You in Ranger?*, claimed Parrish was a bodyguard to a Texas governor. This is the only source for this, but it suggests a prior connection with Pa Ferguson.

It is known that Ferguson formally requested Parrish be made a captain in the Texas Rangers, stating Parrish would be "exceedingly valuable for special work." Adjutant General Hutchings resisted, pointing out the governor could only appoint four captains, which he had already done. Instead, Parrish was offered a position as a Regular Ranger and ordered to report, but failed to do so. Despite never working a day and being processed out in two weeks, he advertised himself as a former Ranger for the rest of his life, exploiting the title's prestige.

This makes a 1917 Waco interview confusing until we realize the only source of the information was Parrish himself. It's highly positive, claiming Parrish was beloved and made "almost daily arrests of slackers [draft dodgers] and agitators [political opponents]." Parrish even told of capturing German subversives, calling it "the most important catch since war broke out." He claimed the Governor summoned him to Waco. In reality, *Texas Ranger Biographies* indicates he was merely struggling with unpaid bills.

Ranger's Corrupt Chief of Police

The oil boom in Ranger, Texas, started in October 1917. In August 1917, he was still traveling central Texas, picking up random work while pretending to be a Ranger. In 1918, he was farming in Eastland County. Other evidence places him in Taylor, Texas, in Fall 1919, where he was arrested for swindling in October and forfeited bond in November. Perhaps he missed court because he was on his way to Ranger? The December 13, 1919, *Ranger Daily Times* implied he'd been Chief of Police there a month.

Walter Prescott Webb's *History as High Adventure* theorized that booms attract workers first, then criminals. Law and order quickly break down, overwhelming the police. In booms like Ranger's, the urgent need for officers means little vetting; towns might hire criminals themselves. Soon, bullies and extortionists control the streets, on both sides of the law.

This cycle played out in Ranger, where the city officially organized in April 1919, 16 months into the boom. The criminal element was established, and police were corrupt, often taking "fines" to allow gambling and prostitution to continue.

Parrish was a police officer in August 1919 and the Chief by December 1919. Mid-December 1919 papers mention a clampdown on a "certain long-fingered gentleman's" gambling establishments. Boyce House claimed he ran a crime boss named Quantrell out of town. That name is probably fictionalized. Parrish himself was out of town for over three weeks during this time, making his responsibility in the crackdown on crime unlikely.

By December 1919, citizens demanded action. Through December and into January 1920, Parrish proclaimed efforts to stop bootlegging and gambling, but by late January, disillusionment set in. He was called to the Board of Commissioners on January 27th to explain his failures; some suggested his resignation. He was put on 15 days' probation. The *Ranger Times* on the 28th ran a negative editorial. Editor Larry Smits was arrested later that day.

The *Ranger Times* on January 29th dedicated its front page to articles against Parrish, alleging false arrest to intimidate Smits. They asked why Parrish met with six cabaret owners in his home to explore ways to legally restrain county officials from closing the cabarets—a clear conflict of interest.

Parrish was already struggling to create the impression that he was working on the side of the law when the Volstead Act took effect on January 17, 1920. Parrish's decline was steep after that. On April 18, 1920, he was arrested by his own deputies for operating a 90-gallon still. He frequently arrested bootleggers, creating little suspicion that he was their supplier. His scam was to sell liquor, arrest bootleggers, confiscate liquor, and sell it again. He exploited every situation.

When informant Jimmy Hubbard tried to stop Parrish, he was brutally beaten with a wet rope. Parrish's chilling response: "Hubbard got what he deserved, and others will get the same dose." Parrish was charged with aggravated assault, but as usual, it went nowhere.

The Parrish Family and Final Decline

His problems escalated, yet he attempted to regain control, joining the Chamber of Commerce in April and closing cabarets in June, but by the end of June, it was over for him. The last sight of him in Ranger was on July 8th, signing paperwork for his last property over to his mother and sister. He simply walked away, leaving his troubles and facing no immediate consequences.

Nepotism was blatant in the story. Parrish's sister, Blannie Malone, his brother, Buck, and mother, Margaret, all benefited from his position. Blannie's story was even more compressed than Byron's. She was officially identified as the mounted humane officer when the City Pound opened on December 23, 1919. It was a full-time police position with the same pay as other police officers. On December 29th, the *Ranger Times* reported her "seriously sick." On December 30th, Officer R.L.

Chambers took over the pound, and Blannie was never heard of again in that capacity. One wonders how long she was paid after working only four days, including Christmas.

Other Parrishes made news. Byron's brother Buck was also on the Ranger Police force and was later arrested for assault with a gun and highway robbery. The Parrish Brothers, Byron and Buck, had a typewriter-repair and piano-tuning business. His mother, Margaret Ann (M.A.) Parrish, owned downtown lots and a dray service. Interestingly, five teamsters from a rival dray company were arrested for operating without a license—a clear maneuver to support his mother. The accusation was false.

While Parrish was not brought to justice for criminal activities in Ranger, his life did spiral. After fleeing Ranger under indictment in July 1920, he briefly stopped in Hale County, where he was arrested for making and trafficking liquor. He was found guilty on August 24th, 1921, and sentenced to two years in prison. The case was reversed and dismissed on appeal, leaving him free to return to New Mexico—to beat up his wife.

Even while fleeing Ranger and under indictment in Hale County, he married his third wife, Bennie, in September 1920. Before a year passed, he was jailed for domestic violence, leaving behind his 19-year-old wife and five-week-old baby. He was 46. While he was in jail, Bennie discovered Parrish had an affair with her stepmother. Bennie's reaction was tragic: she beat the woman to death with a claw hammer. Despite this high drama, Parrish and Bennie had a second child in 1923, before divorcing in time for him to marry another woman in 1925.

His public record quieted for a few years, with more marriages and children. By November 1930, his life was still spiraling, marked by a drunk driving accident in San Angelo.

For his tragic death, we go to McCamey and Rankin in Upton County. The *Fort Worth Star-Telegram* announced his death respectfully; the *Abilene Reporter-News* was harsher, stating he "dropped dead at the county jail." His newborn daughter, Ruby, had died a week earlier. Unable to manage adult life, he drowned his sorrow in alcohol, leading to his final arrest. He was so intoxicated that he ultimately died of alcohol poisoning in the jail. He was 55, leaving six children from age two to 24.

Byron Parrish was a colorful individual, but not in the celebrated Boyce House way. He was a bully, an abuser, an alcoholic, an extortionist, and a swindler. He often worked within the law, performing paid tasks, but he knew how to exploit situations. After familiarizing himself with a community's dark side, he would immerse himself in it.

While we celebrate our Texas Rangers, no organization is perfect. Parrish's affiliation with the Rangers was tenuous at best, but he exploited it his entire life, using the automatic trust generated by the title to garner undeserved respect. Without that short interlude making him seem more impressive, he turned out to be just another drunk living in drama.

THE SHALOMA

An excerpt from the novel *East of Eeden 1: The Shaloma* by Shann Tajiah

Chapter One

Javicia hiked her backpack higher against her shoulders, trying to ignore the burning of her thighs as she was driven further into the wilderness. The chants and screaming of the crowd that had lined the streets on Constania were days behind them, but the march through the flatlands had done nothing to keep them from haunting her. They were only hours away from the ocean now, where her companions had been instructed to abandon her to the elements or whatever fate awaited her there.

Her lips twisted bitterly. Whatever joy she had found in returning to the town of her childhood had been quickly stifled by the fear and hatred that her visions brought no matter where she had fled over her twenty-seven years. Now, after she had warned the city that they would be destroyed if they acted on their plans to invade the lands of Eeden, she had been banished, and worse of all, branded a witch.

Her eyes burned, and she fought not to rub them. The sign of witchcraft had been branded into the whites of her eyes with needle and ink, and while it had not been too painful, it had been terrifying. She imagined her green irises looked even more striking now that the whites of her eyes were stained black. Regardless, there was no way for her to hide the judgment from anyone who would look upon her.

At least her tongue had been spared. It was only the city leaders' fear that she spoke the warnings of the Most High that had delivered her from that punishment.

Her prayers for healing had been left unanswered. Though she felt His voice whispering reassurance to her battered spirit, she couldn't help but embrace the feelings of rejection that shadowed her thoughts.

They paused for a moment and Javicia stood looking over the expanse of Adamah as she tamed her unruly red hair with a scrap of fabric she had torn from her tunic. The golden light of the daystar cast shadows over the dunes of rock and sand.

Javicia took the opportunity to re-moisten the pad that she had soaked with an herbal tincture and pressed its coolness to each eye in turn, wishing she could just close them and rest a while.

The men surrounded her tightly again, coming just close enough that her skin itched with the need to cringe from the condemnation they radiated. Their superstitions keeping them just out of her reach so she couldn't touch them accidentally or otherwise. A wry smile graced her face for a moment as they used their staffs to prod her along, their fear evident under their masks of anger and disgust.

Two more days passed in a blur of aching muscles and exhaustion. The stretch of desert slowly gave way to the beaches of the Dalis Ocean. The men quickly made camp, and Javicia sank gratefully to her knees as she let her pack fall from her aching back. She unrolled her sleeping mat before choking down the warm water and tough jerky she was given. The men settled into their own mats, one sitting to keep watch. He stared openly at her, but she ignored him, caring for her eyes before wrapping a length of cloth around her head to protect them from any blowing sands.

The daystar was just beginning to set, the rising of the nightstar that dimly lit the skies still hours away, but fatigue felt like a fog over her mind. Despite her screaming muscles and the itchy feeling beneath her eyelids, Javicia fell asleep instantly.

It was the sound of screaming that woke her, and she froze beneath her blanket her heart pounding so hard that it felt like her body was rocking from side to side. The cloth around her eyes had slipped away, and she cracked her lids slowly.

She forgot to breathe as a large shadow separated from the shade of the nearby cliffs. The muted starlight cast long shadows, and a pit formed in her stomach as she watched a four-legged creature leap upon one of the men as he tried to run from the camp.

More shadows moved until one by one, each of the men were reduced to unmoving heaps on the sand.

Javicia's hands shook, and she tried the quiet the gasping sounds that escaped her throat as her instincts warred between playing dead or fleeing. Her body froze when a growl sounded beside her, and she was cast into shadow.

Stupid puny humans.

Time stilled. The sense of his voice warming her even as the purring cadence made her instinctively press back against the ground in fear. A sequence of images flashed in the back of her mind and the voice returned.

Why does this one not run? A cold nose pushed at her cheek roughly.

It has fear, but also strength. Listen, another replied, and they all stood silently for a few moments as her heart continued to race.

Javicia squeezed her eyes close as a paw raised above her head. A desperate prayer screamed through her mind, "Abba! Not like this!"

The blow never came. Instead, the cold nose returned, this time gently nudging her neck until she opened her eyes. The beast's breath huffed gently against her ear as it continued to nudge her until her limbs loosened.

Uncertainly, wondering if she was dreaming, Javicia slowly stood to face the pack of animals that stood around her. She could feel their curiosity and a strange thread of joyful recognition as they whisper-thought to each other on what felt like the edge of her mind.

She looked at them in turn, the nightstar illuminating them enough for her to judge their size, but nothing else. Four of them sat staring back at her with cocked heads, their tall ears turned toward her intently, while the other remained at her shoulder. Her head began to throb as their foreign thoughts began to crowd into her head, growing louder as their excitement grew.

Javicia squeezed her eyes tightly closed as she raised her fists to press against her temples. A chattering sound came from the animal standing beside her and the mental pressure faded. She sighed in relief as one by one the others rose and left the camp.

The remaining beast sat in front of her, and the tickle of his curiosity was so strong that it began to awaken her own about him and his companions.

Tiny she-human, no more fear. ***Come.***

She gasped under the weight of the command, understanding the dominance he wielded over his pack with that one word. A heat rose in her chest and not knowing why or how, she resisted, somehow understanding that she could not surrender her will to his. She slowly turned to face the animal that towered over her.

It was hard to comprehend what he looked like as the nightstar played peek-a-boo with the clouds, but she knew that when he had been standing beside her, she had barely passed his shoulder.

She had never seen a creature so large, but he reminded her of the bedtime stories her grandmother had told about the great guardians of Eeden. A creature that was so large and territorial that no one knew the secrets Eeden held.

She unconsciously rubbed her arms as a chill spread over her skin. What would make such a frightening creature stop its paw in mid-strike?

Javicia tore her eyes away, turning her attention back to the camp. She flinched as her gaze skimmed over the unmoving mounds of the men. The alpha beast seemed to sneeze in disgust as she took in the state of the camp and the men's violent deaths.

Pups safe now. Shaloma is safe. Roux sent them away.

She shuddered under the emotion that accompanied his statement, wondering when she would be sent away too, then jumped as he sent up a screaming howl that chilled her blood.

The Shaloma is safe now! Come!

She stepped forward haltingly, deciding not to try him further. She forced her breathing to slow, focusing instead on her task as she knelt and gathered her things quickly and flung her pack to its place over her shoulder.

A part of her was certain that she would be reduced to a heap in the sand, but the still small voice in her heart whispered encouragement, and she grasped at it.

She followed the one that called himself Roux through the camp. Her gut twisted as she passed the fallen men, pausing only to collect two water bladders and a knife that had fallen in the attack. She slipped the short blade into her belt, feeling a fissure of comfort even though it would be ineffectual against the size of the beasts.

Roux made a chattering sound, his annoyance flowing through their strange link. *Foxkin, not beasts.*

"Sorry," she said, feeling chastised beneath his eavesdropping. "I've never met Foxkin before, and you are rather large and beastlike."

Roux chuffed, and it sounded remarkably like a laugh. *Come tiny Shaloma, my mate waits.*

He turned and walked down the beach, and Javicia paused, considering if she should follow. The clouds blocked the nightstar's dim light and she resigned herself to follow, knowing her chances of survival on her own were slim.

She was tempted to look back towards Constania, but there was nothing left but death for her there, so she set her shoulders and followed Roux.

Chapter Two

They continued in the same direction that the men had been taking her, north along the shores. As they moved along, the other Foxkin began to fall in ranks around her. The edge of her mind tingled with their conversation, the images they sent back and forth creating short bursts of language in her mind.

She was intrigued as she listened and considered that legends of a time when humans had understood the beasts of the air, sea and land may have been more than just tales to lure tiny ones to sleep.

Their emotions flowed through her as they conversed, some excited, others clearly concerned by her presence among them. Her attention turned back to them as the tone of their conversation seemed to sharpen.

Leave it behind, it slows us down with two legs, a distinctively male voice said.

No! We found her, bring her home! A softer, more feminine voice replied.

It's afraid of us; it's broken. It's not the right one. Leave it to die, a different male countered.

Their discussion of her finally dwindled in the early morning. They had kept her moving through the night, the wet sand dragging at her every step. The beach had narrowed until they had to walk single file between crashing waves and red cliffs that jutted high above their heads. Javicia looked longingly at each cave that the waves had carved into the rock, but the pack urged her on until they reached one of their liking.

Javicia's head hurt more from their conversation than her body ached from the hours of travel and lack of sleep. She paused frequently to tend her eyes as they began to swell closed. She sighed with relief as the cool darkness welcomed them, and she didn't resist as Roux used his nose to nudge her deeper and deeper into the depths.

She buried her hand into his soft fur to steady herself in the darkness, feeling his shoulder shift beneath her fingers as she stumbled beside him. She sank down with him when he stopped to lie down, letting her body settle heavily against him.

Sleep now.

Her body shuddered with a sigh of relief as one by one the Foxkin fell asleep around her. Two kept watch, but their minds quieted, focused only on the sounds and smells around them.

Roux curled up around her; his fur warm and silky against her skin. She slowly relaxed as the heat of his body completely enveloped and protected her from the damp coldness of the cavern. She felt his tail settle over her as she drifted to sleep, feeling safer than she had in years.

* * *

Cover Copy for *East of Eeden 1*: *The Shaloma*

Banished from society and branded a witch, Javicia is left to die at the hands of the elements or the savage beasts that guard the borders of Eeden.

The Foxkin have been guarding Eeden's secrets for generations, but the humans have become fearless and are willing to risk everything to discover what the beautiful forest hides.

Called by the Most High to stop the conflict, Javicia hides among the Foxkin, determined to leave humanity to its fate. But when the safety of those she loves is thrown into the balance, will she choose survival or sacrifice?

SHOOTING STARS

Steve Denehan

Between one Halloween and another
we find a pack of sparklers
bring them out
into the late summer evening, and
look at each other

I offer the lighter to my daughter
ask if she would like to get them going
she shakes her head

I don't want to burn my fingers.
You won't.

she takes it from me, slowly
puts her thumb on the sparkwheel
pulls it down
nothing
with my eyes I tell her
Try again.

a spark, a flame
she moves the sparkler to it
we wait
one second, another
a micro explosion
a little scare and then
wonder

I light mine from hers and we hold them steady
magic in our hands
her face aglow
from the pinprick fire
her face aglow from within

we move them in the warm dark
tracing patterns on the air
our initials
spirals
hearts

we make sure to throw them
just before they burn out
that they might trace an arc across the sky
that they might never land

DREAM VACATION

A Memoir Essay by Linda Gordon

***Vacation**, n. Freedom or release from some regular activity; a period of suspension of study, work, or regular duty, as for travel, recreation, or relaxation.*

The ideal model of a dream vacation for many is only for R and R, rest and relaxation. Passive words, conjuring images of lying on the beach as the sun melts tight muscles into jelly, and bringing home only a sunburn, a few seashells, and hitchhiking grains of sand.

This year's vacation was nothing like that. R and R did not seem to be part of the package as three generations arrived in the mountains from five different states, bringing bicycles, kayaks, fishing gear, hiking sticks, and games to fill up four condominiums. Four siblings and their spouses, all except one on the north side of sixty, seven children and three spouses, all in their thirties, and five grandchildren, ages eight to twelve, were all mixed together for four days. Some had not seen each other for years. If one of the R's stood for recreation, then yes, we had that covered.

And yes, it was a period of suspension from study, work, or regular duty, as well as from the outside world. We all played, and many played hard, as we picnicked and fished, hiked and biked, paddle boarded and rafted, ate like kings and like pigs, then played games at the end of the day. We went shopping, briefly, to buy T-shirts and caps, and I thought those and pictures would be all that we would be taking away, until the last night before we were scheduled to leave.

After supper that night, two of our family that play guitar and bass guitar, but had never played together, set up their instruments and portable amp outside the back door of the main condo. The rest of us circled our lawn chairs in the grass. The musicians were talented and entertaining, but this was not a passive vacation, so it wasn't long before seniors were dancing with the grandkids. It was then that I began to recognize the freedom and release part of the vacation. Not only from work, but from the ordinary days of our lives that may not hold us back, but do not move us forward. The inhibitions that we place on ourselves were still strong in the thirty something crowd, remaining seated, even as their kids asked them to dance. Soon the young ones moved on to tapping spoons to make a surprisingly rhythmic addition to the songs. The four senior sisters and sister-in-law perched on a knoll, like birds on a wire, impulsively felt the need to choreograph a *Charlie's Angels* routine, changing the lyrics from "secret agent man" to "secret aging man" as the guitars played on. One of the young ones played air guitar after joining the musicians on the porch, putting on a show so funny that he could have taken it on the road. The senior brother attempted to sing "Hotel California," knowing only the chorus and not having nearly a high enough range and one of the senior sisters grabbed a blanket to run through the crowd with the blanket flying behind to "Ghost Riders in the Sky." The youngsters were still too young to have inhibitions, and the seniors were now secure enough to just have fun, laughing even more as they realized that they were still able to embarrass their kids.

Then one in the group of thirty-year-olds pushed past her fear of singing in public (for the surrounding condos had opened their windows and doors) and sang a solo of "Let it Be." The clowning all stopped and there was only the sweet, clear music rising in the mountain air as the sun was setting.

It was then that I thought of the faces of the four flatlander cousins that had peeled away from the other hikers to follow a much steeper and more difficult trail. Their shining faces in the selfie when they made it to the top spoke volumes. And the two cousins who took a 5:30 a.m. hike to see the sun rise and then slip into the freezing water to look out from the back of a waterfall surely came out changed.

When it got dark enough for the stars to appear, we all stood close together to sing all four verses of "Amazing Grace," a fitting final song for the gift of a vacation that had bound us all together, while releasing us at the same time.

HOOKED

A Short Story by Robert Workman

He drank white tequila and water, straight-up, at the bar of *Los Lobos del Norte* until Manolo, the bartender, asked if he'd had enough. He grabbed the bottle and poured another one, a tall one.

He was haunted by her long silhouette, her dark eyes, the scent of her body and the soft, warm touch of her skin. Off the coast of Cuba, they had lain together as waves lapped the sides of their sailboat. They made love in their hotel shower in the morning and at sunset in the waves off the beach. She said love is nature's aphrodisiac. She said a lot of things.

As a boy, he surpassed his peers as a local fisherman. Early one morning, he snuck out with his father's big lures to the sunrise fog of the forbidden pond where big pikes lurked. When he miscast, a hook impaled the web of his hand between his thumb and forefinger.

His mother assured him that his father was not just a doctor, he was an expert in fishhook removal. He had removed fishhooks from every part of the body, including a woman's eye. Because she was his mother, he trusted her; he believed her.

His father had him lie on the couch. He asked him to turn away. As he closed his eyes and smelled the stale fabric of the couch cushion, his father's grip on his hand felt reassuring. He felt the slight jolt of the clippers when his father snipped the barb off the hook. He waited to feel the sensation of the metal sliding smoothly out of his palm.

Suddenly, his heart slammed against his ribcage. A burst of omnipresent white light flashed. He shrieked at the ripping of his flesh, the blood, the shock. He screamed his pain at his father, his hurt at his mother. His father said it was the only way. His mother handed him his first shot of whiskey.

* * *

That morning, he awoke to see the silhouette of the woman as she stood in the window against the brazen sunlight of a hot summer morning. He smelled the fabric of the sheets. She took his hand in a touch that was tender, reassuring. She told him she was leaving; he would not see her again. She asked him to turn away.

He drank white tequila and water, straight-up.

AN INFANTRY MEDIC I'LL REMEMBER FOREVER

A Memoir Essay by Robert B. Robeson

As a soldier in the service of America during time of war, it's not always possible to do exactly what you want in life. Yet you do what you must. Not every act of heroism and courage is marked by a monument. Many exist only in the memories of those who were there. That's why today, over 55 years later, one special infantry medic's memory is still fresh, compelling, and painful. Vivid memories of him often return like "phantom pains" felt in limbs long ago lost. As William Makepeace Thackeray so aptly stated, "Bravery never goes out of fashion."

In late January of 1970, I was a captain, a US Army Medical Service Corps pilot, and operations officer during the Vietnam War. My assignment was to the 236th Medical Detachment (Helicopter Ambulance) located at Red Beach on the southern shore of picturesque Da Nang Harbor. I'd assigned myself to a week of duty with three other medical evacuation crew members at our field-site aid station at Landing Zone Hawk Hill, 32 miles south of Da Nang along Highway 1.

My flight medic had become a close friend with an infantry medic who belonged to a company co-located with us there. Midway through the week, my medic mentioned that his friend wanted to meet me. He'd heard I was a published writer. Writing happened to be one of his interests, too.

There was heavy enemy action in our operational area during this time. One hectic afternoon, between our medevac missions and those of his infantry company, my medic arranged a meeting in the battalion aid station. I remember his friend was 19 years old. Physically, he wasn't someone you'd expect to find on the offensive line of the NFL Denver

Broncos. He was short and slight. But I soon discovered that God had put more into him than anyone could tell from the outside.

We stood together out of the steady stream of traffic near the entrance next to the radio shack. Wounded patients were being carried in on bloody stretchers from another medevac helicopter out of Chu Lai, to the south. We quietly talked about writing and flying for about 20 minutes before another mission was called in and my crew had to scramble.

During our brief conversation, this young man barely out of high school—whose name I can't recall after all of these years—looked up squarely into my eyes. He held my gaze for a long moment before speaking words I haven't forgotten.

"Sir," he said, "when you get back to 'the World,' tell them what it's like here. Tell them what we're trying to do."

At that moment, his speech seemed to be more intense than the situation called for. I was thinking that if he wanted to be a writer, this should be a goal of his own.

"I will," I replied without further comment. We shook hands again before I hurried outside to where my copilot had already fired-up our jet-powered aircraft.

The devastating news reached me, a week later, in operations at our unit headquarters in Da Nang. That's when I remembered my momentary interaction with this brown-haired infantry "Doc." His platoon had been out on patrol when they were ambushed by a much larger enemy force. Their "point man" had been seriously wounded and became separated from the rest of his platoon. The platoon leader, a lieutenant, ordered them to fall back in an attempt to regroup. The point man could be heard screaming for "Doc" above the ensuing firefight.

Everyone was aware that in this type of guerrilla warfare North Vietnamese Army troops would often not kill a wounded American.

They'd use him to lure other Americans back into the kill zone. They knew how highly we prized life. Enemy fire continued unabated. He was warned not to approach his wounded comrade until reinforcements arrived and artillery could be called onto enemy positions. That's when this teenage medic began removing his web gear.

"My job is to get to him," he said to those nearby. "I'm going. He shouldn't have to die alone."

He set down his gear and weapon and only kept his aid bag. Then he crawled about 50 meters back through the confusion, chaos, and enemy fire to his wounded buddy trapped between the opposing forces. That's where he was later found, with his arm around his friend. Both were dead. They'd been executed at close range. Neither of them had been close to a weapon. They passed from this life together. Somewhere in the Que Son Valley southwest of Da Nang in I Corps, their souls took flight. Only God knows what happened between them in their final moments on Earth.

I believe he knew he was going to die that afternoon. His commitment to a fellow American, though, held a higher priority. That's why he left his weapon behind and any opportunity to defend his patient or himself. He didn't want it falling into enemy hands, too. He chose not to cast his lot with the survivors. A wounded comrade facing a lonely and painful death needed him more. For this reason, their lights in our troubled world were quickly extinguished.

I believe that brief time with this young man in the aid station, when he stared into my eyes and spoke those words, was his way of telling me he might have had a premonition that he wasn't going to make it. In the Bible, Jesus said it best in John 15:13 (King James Version): "Greater love hath no man than this, that a man lay down his life for his friends."

They awarded him a Purple Heart and a posthumous Silver Star, America's third highest medal for heroism. Yet he'd given us so much more. He lived a short, violent life attempting to help others and was subsequently buried somewhere in the land he loved with little fanfare.

Many futile years were spent in an attempt to track down my flight medic who'd introduced us. A concerted effort was made to discover the name of this infantry medic by his approximate date of death through various military units and organizations, but without success.

Memories of unflinching, head-on heroism in combat die slowly for those who have witnessed it. I now know that courage can only be measured by its own yardstick. It's not calculated by size, sex, or race, but rather by deed.

There's an old saying, "Don't let a man be known for the last thing he does. Let him be known for the best thing he does." Sometimes, as in this medic's case, the best thing *was* the last thing.

Today time ticks remorsefully on. Yet whenever I think back to all of the brave young men and women I was privileged to know and fly with in combat, he heads the list. He gave all he could ... and more. Now he belongs to eternity—one complete cycle beyond our vision.

I was fortunate to have had the opportunity to know him, if only briefly. I'll remember forever this supreme sacrifice made by a unique American patriot who will never be with us again in this life. And I thank God and his parents for lending him to America, if only for a short 19 years.

LOVE IN THE DARK

Priscilla Bettis

My dear,
I love to love you most at night
when the leaves on trees
are shadowed assemblies suspiring
with each stir of summer air,
when the old farmhouse
is as much a granite monolith
as a clapboard abode,
when your eyes are umbral
and your lips are void.
It is at this time
we walk hand-in-hand
without a stumble,
for the light within you,
brighter than day,
illumines our path.

GRIT

A Short Story by Ruth V. York

Hattie turned from the washpot wearily, wiping grimy moisture from her face. The lone mesquite behind her adobe house cast a thin shade over her, and a wispy wind stirred the tight silver curls about her ebony face. It had blown such a gale last evening. Grit was over everything.

It was impossible to escape the grit in this land, she thought. But that was as needs be. A person needed a lot of grit in his craw to last out here. She thought of Jake.

Behind her the washpot of tallow popped softly as bubbles rose to the surface. She straightened the wicks dangling from several short withes cut from salt cedars and now hanging in the forks of the mesquite. No doubt these candles would be gritty like the last batch. They burned the same, but they brought less in Jake's butcher shop. Heaven knew they needed every penny.

Hattie heard the muffled fall of hooves across the parade ground, and by long habit her heart leaped. A platoon of buffalo soldiers was returning from patrol. They were still too far away to recognize faces, but of course Ben's was not among them. She sighed and glanced toward the stone bakery on the south side of the compound.

Ben stood at the bakery door, his right shoulder pressed against the door frame, watching the soldiers approach. His left forearm, straight before him, rested on his crutch.

Several soldiers saluted smartly as they passed him. He straightened, returning the salutes.

As the last soldier passed, Ben slowly placed the crutch under his arm, turned, and hobbled back to the scorching ovens.

Hattie watched, her heart twisting between pride and sorrow. A movement caught her eye. Jake had come out the back door to watch, too.

He turned. The same pain and pride warred in his eyes. He walked over and lifted her chapped hands to his lips. Then he wrapped her in his arms, rocking her gently to and fro.

"He's *alive*, Hattie," he murmured softly. "We got to remember that. He's *alive*."

REMEMBERING - A POEM ABOUT DEMENTIA

Steve Denehan

The phone rings
it is my father
I enjoy our chats
though these days
he often mentions
that he has not seen me
for a long time
even though
we might have visited
the day before

these days
he often mentions
that he has no recollection
of the previous day
or week
that he cannot remember
what month it is or whether
it is morning
or evening

these days
feel longer
than they should, and
I hate myself for wishing
that, even for a while
I could forget about it all

THE CASE OF THE SKELETAL REMAINS OF A TEXAS RANGER LOST ON THE BATTLEFIELD OF ESKOTA

A Column by Linda Spetter

I wouldn't call my father an out-and-out liar, but he has spun a few wild tales in his day. Growing up on a farm in Eskota, Texas, I was introduced at an early age to the fine art of telling tall tales.

The sprawling community of Eskota is located approximately halfway between Merkel and Sweetwater, and it abounds with pastures, creeks, gullies, Indian artifacts and rattlesnakes. My father and I often roamed these acres hunting arrowheads or visiting the former Indian campsites, and all the while my father concocted wildly outrageous tales which I—poor innocent—accepted as gospel truth.

Under his spell, a washed-out hole in the ground would turn into a Promised Land where prospectors once dug for gold. He would dramatically recreate the scene before me, showing exactly how the fortune hunters had counted off the paces from that tree to arrive at precisely the spot where this washed-out hole in the ground was.

For years, whenever I passed that old hole, my eyes would glitter with the vision my father had created for me.

On one of our expeditions, I found an old, rusted pen-knife which my father promptly identified as one he had lost 20 years earlier while plowing. (Let's see, that would have made him approximately seven years old at the time.)

The greatest adventure of all was the one which I have mentally dubbed, "The Case of the Skeletal Remains of a Texas Ranger Lost on the Battlefield of Eskota."

It all began, innocently enough, as my father and I were picking pecans along the creek. Suddenly he froze in his tracks, and it was clear to me that something tragic was about to unfold.

"There," he whispered, pointing to a bleached-out bone which looked suspiciously like the hind quarter of a dead cow.

"This appears to be the hip-bone and leg of a man," he solemnly announced. Accordingly, I drew in my breath.

Then (what luck!) he reached over and picked up a rusty, dirty metal disc. A star was carved out in the center of the disc, and the word TEXAS was inscribed in a circle around the edge.

"He must have been a Texas Ranger," Dad said. "This bone and this badge is all that's left."

It was all very logical. The man's body was pointing down toward the creek, which was why the skull and torso had washed away.

"How did he die?" I asked.

"He must have been scouting down the creek for Indians when a gang of Bluecoats jumped him and cut his gizzards out."

Within minutes, my father had transformed a bone and a badge into one of the goriest murders of the Civil War.

What excitement! What a story to tell my friends at school! I told my fifth-grade teacher, Mrs. Joy Carmichael, and she was so enchanted that she had me hold up the medallion and tell the whole class (a 1960 version of Show and Tell).

I even went so far as to tell the school principal, Jerry Bob Smith, and I could see that he was impressed.

I told Dad to let the newspapers know, and I think I considered writing a letter to *Life Magazine*, but it must have slipped my mind.

Several years later I was passing through my father's room when by chance I noticed a metallic object gleaming on the chest of drawers.

The Texas Ranger badge! I turned the badge over in my hand, fondly recalling the memories it evoked.

What impressed me most, however, was the quality of the badge. It was the type that comes out of bubblegum machines.

THE BILLY BUDD INCIDENT, *OR* THE HANDBASKET EXPRESS

A Mostly True Memoir by Jennifer Neville Maddle

Some years ago I read those *Left Behind* books—you know, the ones about Armageddon and Judgment Day. Now, I don't know a rational person who has read those books and not had some pretty serious thoughts about the Great Hereafter. The whole point of those books, as I see it, is that when Judgment Day comes around, we all better be right with the Lord, or pardon the expression, there'll be "hell to pay." And as with any good story, even the Bible, it all boils down to a classic struggle between GOOD and EVIL. That's a pretty big concept if you think about it ... and I do. A lot. I'm not ashamed to say that it scares the bejeezus out of me to think about stuff like that. What if I am "left behind" as a result of my sinful ways, slothful lifestyle, or just plain ol' apathy? So, like I said, it makes you want to get right with the Lord.

My experience with religion is one of the things I hold near and dear to my heart. I think of myself as a spiritual person and open minded to an annoying degree. Like the song says, "Jesus is just alright with me," but then again, so is Buddha and Muhammad, Allah, and all the rest. In my mind, religion is a veritable smorgasbord of ideals, beliefs, opinions, and attitudes. I embrace the fact that what may be right for me may not be right for someone else (and vice versa). Some people, though, would see that as lack of faith or say that I am religiously confused. And my response to them would be this: How could I *not* be religiously confused? As a child, I had two grandmothers doing constant battle over my immortal soul, one a self-proclaimed devout Southern Baptist and the other a Watchtower-wielding Jehovah's Witness. Now, I'm not sure how that stacks up against anybody else's experiences, but in my recollection, it was daily an epic battle of Biblical proportions. Some of my earliest childhood memories of the Baptist Granny were versed with her strict warnings to behave myself because "Jesus don't love ugly little girls" and later warnings to beware all the "devilment" in the world. These were matched only by the Jehovah's Witness Grandmother warning my mother that if we didn't mend our sinful non-Jehovah ways, we'd all end up "swimming in a sea of blood." My mom's reply was that my grandmother was wrong—none of us knew how to swim. Maybe I'm jeopardizing my immortal soul to say this, but that's good stuff.

Growing up, my two best friends were Catholic. I should have known I was in trouble when they explained to me about giving up something for Lent. I guess I just couldn't understand that sort of sacrifice. In my heart of hearts, I was sure that had I been Catholic, I could've convinced everyone that giving up lima beans would've been hard for me. Maybe I just really didn't get it. My friends wouldn't have ratted me out about the lima beans ... so is something really a sin if no one tells on you? Or are we all just on our way to Hell in a Handbasket anyway? I guess in my case, I'd be on the Handbasket Express. And I know this because of a particular incident that happened to me back in high school.

By the time we were sophomores in high school, my friends and I had established ourselves as the good kids. We were the ones who came to school with smiles on our faces and our homework completed. We were the kids whom every teacher loved. And strangely enough, we really liked our teachers, too. We were all taught at home the value of education, so it never seemed too difficult to put our best feet forward and make something of ourselves. It was the least we could do for our parents, you know? And back in high school, Bob Johnson was everyone's favorite teacher—well, band director, actually—so much that he was affectionately known to us all as Mr. Bob, Band Director Bob. The weird thing was that our sophomore year, Mr. Bob also got to be our English teacher, which was something that we'd never expected, but found pretty exciting. We all loved Bob. He was like a big ol' kid to us, but way cooler than that because he treated us just like we were adults. He would even tell us "dirty" jokes and laugh right along with us. Sophomore year was going to be awesome.

So everything was moving along just fine in almost every class. English was fun—we had just finished reading *The Red Pony* with Bob. But there was one class that wasn't working out so well at all—Mrs. Perry's geography class. We were in the same class as freshmen, and we couldn't have that. So being the good students that we were, we were able to secure a schedule change. We were the good kids—who would say no to us? And who offered us an alternative? Good ol' Bob Johnson, that's who. He had sixth grade band during that period—the last period of the day—but could use the help in keeping his filing up to date. And we were the good kids, the ones he could trust to help out. We would become his Band Aides.

Well, it didn't take long for the whole lot of us to settle into our new class, which we loved, by the way. With it came freedoms that we'd never before imagined. That filing project was really nothing more than a brief diversion for us—my friends and I were much more interested in hanging out in Bob's office and talking on his phone to our college boyfriends while he was teaching the sixth graders. Then one day it occurred to us that we were truly only confined to that office by regulations of our own doing and, of course, the four walls. What a concept—we could leave! My best friend, Nolie, had a car, and Bob wouldn't mind, or at least he'd never tell on us. And besides, we were the good kids. Good kids didn't do bad things, so therefore, who could call this a bad thing? We only wanted a little fresh air anyway, so why not skip last period and go to the lake?

And so we did. And what a rush. I'm not even sure we felt guilty about it—it was just too cool to have our own escape. We played 007 in the parking lot, quickly discovering that big yellow buses make great barriers to hide behind. We were outlaws in our own minds. And that's how it went, at least three days a week for at least a month, right up until Bob went and got all adult on us and told us not to leave anymore. And besides that, English class wasn't so much fun anymore either since he'd chosen a new novel for us to read. *Billy Budd, a Sailor*. What was Herman Melville thinking when he wrote that? And what was Bob thinking to make us read it? We were the good kids. We didn't deserve this. So we plowed into *Billy Budd* with all the enthusiasm of a half dead possum and got nowhere and nothing out of the first set of chapters. But our cries fell on deaf ears with Bob, who, for whatever reason, really seemed to be enjoying *Billy Budd*. I thought perhaps he had always harbored some deep desire to become a sailor himself and was playing it out right before our eyes in the guiles of *Billy Budd*, but my imagination has always leaned toward the dramatic. He was probably just trying to get us to learn something. Poor Bob, if he had only known what evil was about to befall him and Billy Budd.

So now we were back to hanging out in Bob's office during last period after being busted on the lake escapades, and you can only make so many phone calls before it loses its appeal. Someone should have realized back then that a bored teenager is a dangerous teenager, but we were the good kids, so I'm guessing we got the benefit of the doubt. Well, we shouldn't have. What transpired over one class period on one particular day was a series of truly unfortunate events, unparalleled in any universe. Time and space must have collided to make us lose our minds. Or maybe we just used them in such a way as they had never been used before. Or maybe the devil made us do it. Who knows? What I do know is that over the next sixty minutes, my friends and I departed down a path we had never seen before, venturing into the uncharted waters of deceit and soul-jeopardizing sin.

Here's what happened. We were supposed to be reading *Billy Budd* to prepare for our test the next day. Needless to say, none of us were into doing that. Being the naturally curious children that we were, after having lost interest in the book (after about three seconds), we began to innocently browse through the things on Bob's desk. Of course we knew we shouldn't be doing that, but the temptation was just too much. And what did we find? Oh, miracle of miracles—a copy of next day's *Billy Budd* test with an answer key attached! The Lord surely does work in mysterious ways. God himself had surely sent us this answer key; after all, He was undoubtedly aware of our struggles. Now all we had to do was copy the answers and put the test back where we found it. But should we do it? I wish I could say that I remember hesitating or that it was an agonizing decision, but I'm afraid I'd be fooling myself. We copied those answers. But here's where the situation really took a downward spiral. My friend Mel (the really good one, the nicest kid in school) said, "Why write the answers down? He's got a copy machine right there." Oh. My. God. She's an evil genius! If we were going to mess up, we might as well go all the way bad. And so we did. We not only made copies for ourselves, but for everyone in our entire English class—yes, that was us, generous to a fault. And of course we wasted no time distributing the answers back at our lockers immediately after school. Share the wealth, right? And besides, we had some studying to do to memorize those answers.

I guess we all felt pretty smug the next day when we went into English class to take our test. After all, we were going to ace it, no doubt about that. Still, I don't recall the guilt ...

And all was good until the following day when we returned to English class expecting to see the hundreds on our tests and hear Bob's praises for a job well done. As Bob began handing back the tests, I saw the smiles on my friends' faces and smiled to myself, even before I saw my own one hundred, because I knew we had gotten away with our master plan, our grand scheme. But as I basked in the light of my triumphant accomplishment, I began to notice that not every face in the room held such a look. In fact, there were a couple of people who looked downright mad. My curiosity became even more heightened when Bob asked those particular people to speak to him alone in the hall. There was definitely something amiss. Could it have something to do with *Billy Budd*? We would know soon enough.

And here's how it played out. A couple of people in the class had apparently had some trouble reading Bob's handwriting. Not having read *Billy Budd* at all, there was some confusion over one of the answers. For some reason, they had decided that the answer to number seven on the test was "a stone" when it was actually "a star." It's an easy mistake to make, but two papers with the same incorrect answer was enough to arouse Bob's suspicion. To me, that's irony. But I didn't laugh. My friends who got caught got zeros on that test, but they never told on us. I guess they were just grateful for the *opportunity* to pass, because let's face it, they would've failed anyway. No one was reading *Billy Budd*. Maybe a more ethical person would've stood up and admitted what we had done to Bob, but at age fifteen, I wasn't that kind of ethical. I was Judas, betrayer of all mankind. I'm pretty sure we skipped last period and went to the lake that day. It was just too hard to face Bob. And maybe, just maybe, we were starting to feel a bit guilty ...

To make a long story short, we never told Bob. I grew up right beside a Catholic church; you'd think I'd be more familiar with confession. I hear it's good for the soul. But it never happened. It's not like we all took a vow of silence or anything; we just avoided the topic whenever possible. The irony with Bob, however, continued well into my adulthood. When I became a teacher some years later, I taught Bob's son in sophomore English, and Bob once sent me a note that said, "I think you should make Greg read *Billy Budd*." Was this just Bob's way of being funny, or was he taunting me? The torture continued when he ran for and was elected school board president. Now he signed my paycheck every month. The guilt that I never felt as a child was now a living, breathing reminder of my adolescent indiscretions in the form of *Board Director* Bob, who still didn't know my deepest, darkest secret, my trespass against him.

So when is it time to atone for our sins? I recently spoke with one of my friends who was involved in the incident—my partner in crime. I asked her if she thought I should confess to Bob what we had done. I was surprised that she said no. She believed that it would change his opinion of us forever. After all, we were the good kids, and look what we did. But what we did was wrong. I knew it then and I know it now. Does that mean I'll be "left behind"? It's a sobering thought, to say the least. But I'm fairly certain that God sees the big picture and knows that I am many things—"a picker, a grinner, a lover ... and a sinner." So maybe I'm actually not on the fast track to Hell, the Handbasket Express. And maybe, just maybe, if I do make it to Heaven, Bob and I can read *Billy Budd* together.

DARKNESS, LIGHT, REBIRTH

A Prose Poem by Shane Tovar

Unlimited void, never sundial light again, never have happiness, nor shall be a dial worthy of God. Only to find nothingness to never find the truth. Only find the dial a blackhole, and finally you're in the flames of hell. Where you shall suffer forever, you scream in pain and agony. You pray, but none shall come to save you in the inferno. Ten years have passed, then thirty years have passed, then finally one-thousand years. You shall be reborn a butterfly. You fly without care or feeling, just the wind blowing your wings with grace and inner nature. You try to find a flower to feed. But there aren't any flowers to be seen, so now you starve until you fall to the ground and slowly die with no one to save you. After closing your eyes, a light appears. Then you have been reborn as a baby named Alicia, never knowing what was your past life, never knowing what awaits in your future. All you know is to look in a mirror to comb your beautiful, long, blonde hair and wonder when you can find true love. Then one year later your dream comes true, and he loves you with all his heart, so much he kneels and asks you to marry him. You say yes. Then old age gets to you, then death.

BUDGETING YOUR INCOME

An Article by J.V. Lewis

For a long time I avoided the word *budget* because it sounded like something that would take time to do and would not be a worthwhile endeavor. Since then I have learned that there is a very simple method of making your money work for you. If you work for money, why not make your money work for you?

Money is like water. You can either channel it to go where it will do the most good, or you can waste it. The greatest waste of money is indebtedness. When we are in debt, we are helping someone else make their money work for them. It is much easier to stay out of debt than it is to get out of debt.

If we are already in debt, budgeting our income can help us to not only get out of debt, but also to stay out of debt. So my purpose here is to show you a very simple and easy way to set up your budget that anyone with a calculator that does percentages can do. Once your budget is set up, most of the work is done. After that it's a simple thing to follow because you know what you can afford and what you cannot.

Of course, you can only budget your net income because that is all you have access to. What I'm going to show you will work even if your income varies from month to month or week to week. I know that is very important for many. So let's get started!

To begin with, divide your monthly, weekly, or bimonthly net income (depending on when you get paid) into 10 equal parts. Each part will be 10 percent of your net income. Finding 10 percent of your income is very easy to do with the use of your calculator.

Here is an example: Let's say that your monthly net income is $4,589.45, and you get paid once each month. (If you are paid weekly, or by-monthly, the same method applies.) You enter that amount into your calculator and multiply by 10 percent, and the result will be $458.945. There you have your ten percent.

If you wish to check it, multiply that amount by 10. In other words, $458.945 X 10 will equal $4,589.45, the full amount of your monthly net income.

The next thing to do is to find 10 percent of your 10 percent by the same method. Enter $458.945 in your calculator, multiply by 10 percent, and the result will be $45.8945. Since the last two digits (45) are less than 50 we can drop them to make it simple. If they were 50 or more we would go up to the next penny. In this case, the amount with the last two digits dropped is $45.89. If the last two digits were 50 or more the figure would be $45.90.

Note that 10 percent of 10 percent is 1 percent of 100 percent. In other words, $45.89 is 1 percent of $4,589.45. You'll see why this is important shortly.

First, list your expenses that are always the same. That would be things like your house payment (or rent), car payment, insurance, etc. Next, list the variables, allowing adequate estimates for groceries, clothing, entertainment, etc.

Let's say, for example, you list your house payment of $765.00 per month. We know that 10 percent ($458.95) is not enough to cover the house payment. Therefore, we need to determine how many 1 percents we need to add to that 10 percent. One percent is only $45.89, so we can readily see that we are going to need to add more than just one. Let's see if five are enough: 5 X $45.89 equals $229.45, so let's add that to the $458.95 (10 percent). The result is $688.40. That's still not enough so let's try seven times: 7 X $45.89 equals $321.23 now add that to $458.95, and the results are $780.18. That's enough to cover the house payment.

Since our house payment of $765.00 is less than $780.18, we have $15.18 leftover. Now we need to add a new category to put the $15.18

in. We can call it the miscellaneous category (or *misc*. for short.) I will have more to say about it later.

Now we have used all of the first 10 percent and seven of the 1 percents from the second 10 percent for the house payment, and we have three 1 percents left in the second 10 percent.

Let's say the next category is the car payment of $359.65 each month. We are going to use the same principle for budgeting your car payment as we did your house payment.

Since the car payment is less than 10 percent, subtract $359.65 from $458.95 (the third 10 percent): $458.95 - $359.65 equals $99.30. Now $99.30 is more than two 1 percents, so now we have two 1 percents remaining in the third 10 percent (and still three 1 percents left in the second 10 percent). Two 1 percents equals $91.78. Subtract that from the leftover car payment money, $99.30 - $91.78 equals $7.52 to add to the misc. category. By putting the remainder into the misc. category, we are able to keep dealing with complete 1 percents.

We now have $15.18 plus $7.52 in our misc. category which can be used wherever it is needed to fine-tune the budget.

Just for fun, let's say you want to put the three 1 percents that are left in the second 10 percent and the two 1 percents that are left in the third 10 percent into a savings account. Five X 1 percent ($45.89) equals $229.45, a nice amount to set aside each month. That still leaves seven full 10 percents as well as the $22.70 that is in misc. All we need to do now is address each category, using the same method. You will be surprised how much money you have to spend wisely.

We all know that it is a lot easier to get into debt than it is to get out. And when you are in debt, you are paying interest which means you are helping someone else make their money work for them when it could be working for you. This budgeting method allows for an unlimited number of categories. You can have categories for building a savings account, for giving to charities, and for paying off debts.

After you have your budget set up, you should be able to add up the amount in each category plus the amount that is in your misc. category, and the total should be 100 percent of your net income. If it is not, you can fine-tune it until it is.

Setting up your budget is the most time consuming of all. Once it is done, you have your money channeled in such a way as to control your spending, so it is time well spent. When you are on a budget, you will find that your money goes much farther than when you are not.

Remember, the formula is net income multiplied by 10 percent on your calculator. That establishes your 10 percents. Then multiply the 10 percent amount by 10 percent, and that equals 1 percent of your net income. It is all simple arithmetic that anyone can do with a calculator capable of figuring percentages. Once you have determined your 10 percents and your 1 percents, you are good to go.

THE ROOSTER

Shann Tajiah

Abbie kicked at the stubborn latch on the used coop she had found online. "Hundred-dollar piece of garbage," she muttered, irritated that she had sent her brother to pick it up. He obviously hadn't looked it over before forking over her money. He called it "fixable", but it needed a total remodel!

She sighed, resigned to spending more money on her unexpected guest as she abandoned her assault on the worn coop and went to grab her purse.

Hours later, with the help of a smooth-selling employee named Frank, she had made her debit card cry actual tears. She knew she had gone a bit crazy, but her little car had handled the lumber with ease once she had arranged it to stick out the back window.

"I strongly suggest you meet me at my place. I may have made a mistake, but I bought a large part of the lumberyard, and need help fixing this mess of a chicken coop." She said to Tyler's voicemail as she sped home.

Tyler was a good brother and he was already working on removing rotted wood and screwing down shingles when she pulled up.

He grinned at her over his shoulder, "Hey, Sis. Told you it was an easy fix."

She blew a raspberry at him and showed off her purchases as they unloaded the car.

"I hope you kept your receipt." Tyler laughed as he looked over the pile of wood, chicken wire and other odds and ends.

She waved it in his face obnoxiously, "I'm power-tool challenged, not stupid."

The weekend flew by in a haze of splinters, sore limbs, and a few choice words. As the sun set behind her newly renovated coop, it looked like a mini chicken palace painted in oranges and pinks.

"It looks wonderful." Abbie sighed, happy that the task was finally over.

"Sure was a lot of trouble. Maybe next time you find a lost thing, you should give it away," Tyler said as he packed up to leave.

Her new pet strutted around Abbie's legs and paused to crow fiercely. Abbie laughed as she shooed him through the door and into the run. "Surely one rooster isn't too much to handle."

Tyler laughed, "Just wait. You're about to have a bad case of chicken math!"

Abbie will never admit it, but her brother was right.

A VALENTINE FOR VINNY

A Short Story by Robert B. Robeson

Sea gulls swooped, soared, hovered, and maneuvered effortlessly in a light breeze wafting across the remote beach where I'd come to be alone. Distant sails glided along the ocean's horizon. Their usual anxiety-reducing presence seemed totally alien to my current mindset. I opened the valentine again, received in that morning's mail, and reread its emotionally debilitating, handwritten message. The words couldn't have been more despairing, hurtful, and depressing.

* * *

His name was Vinny—Vinny Valez. We'd first met as seventh-graders in the same junior high homeroom. I remember how I'd tried not to stare at him that first day, but his shocking appearance made it nearly impossible to accomplish. He'd been horribly burned in a trailer house fire a few years before. Vinny's face resembled the tread on an old tire that had been rescued from an incinerator. It was covered by grisly shadows and shapes of old scars and skin grafts representing a mute testimony to the catastrophe he'd experienced at such a young age. The skin on his arms and fingers looked like aged bark. His eyes flickered between eyelids appearing as if they'd been worn away by some rough instrument.

Vinny's mother had perished in the same blaze. His father was part of that long migration drifting from state to state working on road construction or harvesting crops. This type of transient life couldn't have been conducive to Vinny's psychological makeup. Moving every few seasons undoubtedly heightened his already protracted agony and caused it to be even more arduous to endure.

It was difficult, almost impossible, to visualize what he must have looked like in the freshness, strength, and innocence of early adolescence. Now he was caught like a mouse in the trap of one of life's most bitter and unforgiving personal dilemmas. No matter how desperately he struggled, he'd never be able to escape this devastating tragedy that had decimated his young life. Physical and emotional circumstances now bound him as tightly as invisible bands of steel.

A few days after he'd first entered our classroom, I'd attempted to initiate a conversation after school by our lockers in the main hallway.

"Hi, Vinny. I'm Amy Anderson. I just want to welcome you to our school and homeroom." I attempted to look into his eyes and avoid the damaged facial features that took center stage in front of me. My gaze must have wavered. His initial comment was direct and spoken in a soft voice.

"Well, Amy, my burns ain't catchin'. You don't have to worry none about them." I'd heard enough sermons in church and listened to my parents and other adults speak about how grief, trials, and sorrows were supposed to develop a person's character. Yet I wondered, in my own youthfulness, if massive suffering hadn't gone too far in Vinny's case.

"If you need help finding your way around school or catching up on any homework," I said, closing my locker door, "feel free to ask me. Moving here in the middle of a school year can't be the easiest thing for anyone to do."

"There's lots of other things harder to deal with than that. You're a cute girl, with long red hair, green eyes, and all. I doubt if you scare little kids in stores or make them scream on the street the first time they see you ... like I do. But thanks, anyway, for offerin' to volunteer your time."

This was a stark truth Vinny no doubt had to deal with more than anyone else. I had no appropriate reply to offer at that embarrassing moment. We parted in silence.

As our school year progressed, each time a new student or substitute teacher arrived, Vinny endured the stares and whispered questions that he may have overheard. This is when I realized that the terrifying fiery ordeal he'd survived hadn't deprived him of the personal courage to put up with enough disgusting gossip and harassment to last anyone a lifetime.

During the following weeks, I learned about some of the callousness various rabble rousers had displayed toward this transfer student they viewed as *different*. A few of them treated him as though he were some sort of Frankenstein monster in the hallways, classroom, and around the campus. I witnessed even older students displaying a weird compulsion to bully Vinny into submission by referring to him as "Crispy Critter" within earshot. They treated him like he was not quite human. It made me angry that being badly burned in a deadly fire could be a recipe by unthinking kids for ridicule, as though he hadn't suffered enough already.

That's when I first stepped in and confronted a small gaggle of these boys before class one day. I'd already observed Vinny quietly walking away under the brunt of their scathing remarks. These were probably catcalls he'd been exposed to before. That didn't mean they still didn't hurt. Hurt bad. Yet there didn't seem to be anything he could do about it. Complaining or crying wouldn't have helped. I sensed he wasn't the type to bring it to the attention of teachers or the school administration anyway. That would have only added more "snitch" drama and antagonism to what he was already experiencing.

"Hey, yeah you, the one who asked Vinny if he washed his face with Agent Orange," I began, "I think you must have eaten a big bowl of stupid for breakfast this morning. You're all acting like two-year-olds by being a part of your childish mini-mob." I got in their faces as though they were idiots ... and they were.

"So, Crispy Critter now has a girlfriend?" another remarked in a snide way.

"You're all insensitive clods," I shot back. "None of you will ever be eligible to be a member of a smart person's club. How does it feel to be smart-alecks and a blight on the landscape? Vinny's suffered more than any of you can imagine or would have the guts to put up with. He's not a freak in a circus sideshow you've paid admission to comment about. You're the freaks of nature. If you want to see something grotesque and awful looking ... take a look in a mirror!" None of them talked back because they knew they were guilty. Everyone else in the hallway had heard me call them out in a loud voice, which obviously embarrassed them further.

I knew Vinny was someone worthy of trust, respect, and love. He'd endured his physical and emotional pain mostly in silence from the adolescent cruelty that often occurs. A short time after I'd confronted these class clowns in the hallway, Vinny surprised me on my walk home after school. He stepped out from behind a tall hedge as I passed by.

"Amy, I heard what you said to those guys earlier," he began. "I'd just turned the corner of the hallway, but your voice was pretty loud. I don't want you havin' to take any guff from anyone 'cause of me. Nobody's ever done that before."

"It wasn't just for you, Vinny. I did it for them, too. Nobody deserves to be treated like that."

"I don't like talkin' about it much, 'cause they'd never understand how it feels." He took a deep breath. His neck and shoulder muscles tightened.

"I think kids being like that is due more to ignorance about real life than anything else. They're still not smart enough to realize how stupid they're acting."

"I'm not really an actual cripple, ya know," Vinny said. "Gettin' burned is what happened to me. It's depressing and hurts to know these scars will never go away ... and I'm only fifteen. There's no cure for what I've got, and life can last a long time for someone like me. So I'm just doin' the best I can to deal with it in my own way."

This was the first time I'd heard him open up even a little bit to anyone else about his circumstance.

"The fire wasn't your fault," I said. "You're strong. None of them could have handled a similar situation, and you also lost your mother at a young age." I'd become well aware that the rest of his life would probably be long on misery.

"My dad turned to drinkin' to ease his pain about me and mom. And us bein' poor, too, and having to move all the time don't help none. I'm not surprised most people don't want to be around me. All I ever wanted was to belong somewhere. Now I'm startin' to accept bein' alone most of the time 'cause of what I look like. The future I'd always dreamed about kind of fell apart in that fire."

He turned and walked away without saying another word. I began to understand how some people often say more through silence than through a lot of talking.

Our homeroom teacher had a policy of having her students exchange valentines on Valentine's Day each year, the week of February 14th. As the day approached, I figured Vinny's father might not have the money to finance this traditional gesture for all of the other kids on his son's behalf. If Vinny brought no valentines, it was possible he wouldn't receive any, either. Then he might suffer the additional humiliation of having to sit there while everyone else received theirs. With this in mind, I went to a variety store and bought the largest valentine they had, with part of my allowance, and wrote a short note on the back. I told him he was special, that God loved him, and that I wanted to be his friend. The words weren't flowery, just short and to the point trying to be encouraging.

I made sure to sit behind Vinny the day the cards were distributed and while our teacher passed out a pack of candy hearts to each of us. This wasn't difficult since there were always four empty desks around him no matter where he sat in class ... those on all four sides of him.

Of the hundreds of valentines accumulated in a box on a table near the door, my over-sized card was the only one addressed to Vinny and dropped on his desk. Looking over his shoulder, I could see his trembling hands as he struggled to open the valentine's envelope with his burned fingers.

"Happy Valentine's Day, Vinny," I whispered into his damaged left ear.

Slowly turning his waffle-iron face to stare at me, he never said a word. I smiled my best smile and held my breath, hoping he'd understand I didn't want to be like so many of our other cruel classmates. This included those who had belittled and shunned him due to his disfigurement. His face never changed expression, but his dark eyes betrayed emotion. They filled with moisture. He quickly glanced away. Vinny had been the subject of cruelty, sarcasm, and abuse for so long that nothing could have brought tears to his eyes but a simple kindness shown.

A two-dollar valentine and handwritten note were Vinny's only reward for a tragic mishap patiently borne. I was sorry, sad, and ashamed at my own moments of personal revulsion in the beginning.

A number of months later, before our school year ended, Vinny and his dad moved away. I never saw him again. Yet every year, near Valentine's Day, I'd receive a unique valentine with just four words on it. The letters never had a return address and the words were always the same. *Thanks for caring—Vinny*. I graduated from high school, college, and then graduate school before joining the U.S. Peace Corps for a number of years. The rest of the time I worked for various other government agencies overseas. I lived and taught in Asia, Africa, and South America, yet the valentines always found their way to wherever I was with the same clockwork regularity as the German train system and the sparrows returning to Capistrano. I wondered how he always knew where I was.

* * *

On the boulder-strewn beach, with the surf crashing and flowing in a consistent rhythm and the scallop-edged crests of the waves glistening, my eyes scanned the valentine's message for the third time. This year it was composed by a different hand. *Vinny passed away last summer in a construction accident. He'd mentioned to me that you were the only one in all of his travels who ever made him feel special. Thank you for your kindness to him so long ago.*

A secret, silent despair swept over me. The little I'd done to help this burned and burdened youngster seemed suddenly blank and suspicious. A few kind words to him, a few scathing words to his teenage antagonists, and an inexpensive valentine with a short note represented a rather tiny investment in another person's existence. Yet it still appeared to have made a positive impression on Vinny as he transitioned from a troubled and relatively short life into another larger world too distant to return from. In this unique realm, no one would ever be startled by his appearance or make fun of him again.

As an adult, I'd traveled and worked around much of our spinning ball of clay in those thirty-odd years since we'd parted. I'd met hosts of people from all walks of life. But I'd never fully appreciated how the smallest gesture of caring could impact another human being suffering through loneliness, frustration, and pain. I'd taught thousands of students in many countries a variety of subjects, yet what Vinny ended up teaching me was one of the most important life lessons of all. Incredible individuals, not merely the most famous, richest, or best looking who populate our world, are capable of touching our souls and compelling us to remember them long after they're gone. Fortunately for me, Vinny Valez was one such person.

URBAN RENEWAL

Jim Wilson

On this Sunday's morning daybreak,
I sit at a knife-signed,
green wooden picnic table
in a two-cacti landscaped mini-city park
on the south shoulder of U.S. Hwy. 90.

My heart laments a residually regal row
of old, tired, main street buildings,
cornice crown chiseled *Adam Sloan 1928*
and enthroned on the highway's north side.
Once essential soul and sinew saving stores—
dry goods for blue jeans, hardware for shovels
and grocery for bread and beans.

Now modern revivals embarrassingly
hawk imported ceramic cats,
twenty yogurt flavors, gourmet chocolates,
bruised books and tacky silver crosses
pinioned to plastered walls.
All stores fester blisters and bunions
of extreme eclectic art for sale.

Though scarred and scuffed
with modern graffiti logo,
the post office survives
with a valiant vestige of dignity
announcing as did the train depot
of long ago—Marathon, Texas
79842

ASSASSINATION ATTEMPT!

An Excerpt from a Thriller Novel by Robert Workman

Chapter 1

Jack

I stepped out of the Metro Diner onto Montgomery Street, snapped on my aviators. Seconds later, I unwrapped them from my ears. A minute after that, clipped them on again. I wished the sky would make up its mind; I had enough indecision swirling in mine.

Helios wrestled with overweight clouds during a morning of vacillant weather in Manhattan's Lower East Side. Warm humid winds mediated between rain-soaked city streets and sun-glazed sidewalks.

At a crosswalk I paused and scrolled through my phone for a mental massage of the usual daily news: alcohol, drugs, murder, rape, terrorism, theft, war. A sheriff's deputy was killed serving a warrant; a military weapons truck was hijacked; the Fort Knox audit of gold reserves was being stalled; and sestercentennial celebrations were in place for the Tall Ships and the Statue of Liberty.

At East Broadway I popped my collar in defense against the mizzle. My head was tilted down, and I observed my boots as they splashed through shallow slicks on the pavements of Grand Street. Up ahead, sporadic precipitation from the heavens accumulated on a sign suspended above me by a cantilever: *Jack's Gym*.

The eponymous placard over the club's glass door was half a century old. Some of its lights still worked. Its excess drizzle flowed down and turned the soft doeskin of my trench coat chocolate brown. I buzzed, stood aside, waited.

The NYPD cruiser and meat wagon double-parked on the street behind me should have told me something. I should have observed, should have noticed. I was a p.i., a Delta op in a previous life; I didn't miss things, especially blatant conspicuous anomalies.

But my head wasn't in New York City. The nation's capital called; I was wanted at home. *Could I live in two cities at the same time?* I needed the routine of a workout to help my body realign the thoughts in my head.

Moments later, a buzzer sounded; the security latch clicked its release. The twenty-seven steps up to the second level always seemed dark, even during daylight in summer. A dust-covered fluorescent light that burned out years ago held its place in its disinterested existence overhead.

The rest of the gym carried out the same theme of decor. Paint peeled from the walls, tired from decades of deliberate neglect. Several absent tiles left dark holes in the pressed-tin ceiling. The solitary source of refreshment was a watercooler, retired from the Greyhound Port Authority Bus Station decades ago.

The boards of the wood staircase creaked beneath the burden of my 243 pounds as I ascended. I passed by staircase walls lined with photos and posters of Jack's celebrated alumni: Mr. Olympia, IBC middleweight champ, Olympic shot putter, WWE tag team champs.

"Jack's Wall of Fame" was a personal project of mine. I posted the photos of the club's alumni for the gym's only owner and employee out of pride and respect. Jack was the real deal. He didn't care about celebrity or about frou-frou amenities. He preferred before/after photos of his street-level clientele. Jack said he didn't *improve* the joint because the improvements he wanted to see were in his clients.

The creaking, uphill trek was a hike I made a thousand times before. Traces of stale cigar smoke, aged for decades in the exposed wood floorboards and walls, greeted my senses. They blended with the scent of sweat equity from Jack's devotees who invested in their muscular development.

As I climbed, I closed my eyes and inhaled the musty aroma that welcomed me back. When I opened them again, my peripheral vision only recognized the existence of the pictures, not their details. What I noticed was—nothing.

There was no sound. No chatter. No weights crashed onto the splintered wood floor. No soulful speedbag rhythms, no heavy bag groans and punches.

Except for the rustle of rain-soaked outer wear and the muffled tones of men's conversations, the place was quiet. At the top of the stairs, I turned and looked into Jack's office through one of his internal windows.

The sight of the homicide lieutenant struck me as oddly out of place. *What's Happy doing here?*

A pedestal stand next to the railing held Jack's daily sign-in ledger. The date on the page: Monday, June 29, 2026. I picked up the ballpoint pen on a chain taped to its side.

When Jack tagged me with the nickname, "Mister Potato Head," I ran with it and made my signature with a simple, illiterate, *X. So, why was my X already logged in ahead of me at 9:15 a.m. this morning?*

Lt. Ralph "Happy" Moynihan half-turned and looked over his shoulder. The cordial neighborhood detective greeted me, obviously hopeful for my input and expertise.

"Oh, no. What the Hell are you doing here?" he asked.

"I live here," I said. "Almost. I work out before I hit the office. What's going on?"

Happy looked at his watch under an arched eyebrow. "Two guys, over there. Came in and found him like that; called it in."

I asked, "Him, who?"

Happy jerked his head toward the office door. The blood drained out of my body, down to my feet. I felt empty, didn't want to move; somehow I stepped across, looked inside.

The old guy was seated in his green shop chair behind his antique partners desk. His upper torso stretched prostrate across it. His hands gripped the far edge of the leather inlaid mahogany as if he clung for his life. Semi-long white hair cascaded off his shoulders onto the opened books and binders beneath his chest.

I didn't want to believe what my eyes told me they saw. I knew who it was, knew damned well who it was.

Jack was my mentor; Jack was my sensei; Jack was my friend.

Jack was dead.

Chapter 2

Happy

Water ran down my clothes and pooled on the worn out floorboards inside Jack's disheveled office. My hands were jammed into my coat pockets, and my absent-minded fingers scratched around for whatever it was they didn't find.

I stood in the office doorway and stared. That wasn't Jack; it couldn't be Jack. He may have been eighty-six, but he was as healthy and strong as a man thirty years younger.

My eyes couldn't turn from the sight of him stretched face down across his desk. I didn't want to look, didn't want to see, but there he was, in front of me: It couldn't be. Jack. Dead.

My favorite place to receive his words of wisdom sat empty before him: a 50s postmodern Western chair, green, with a bas relief bucking bronco stitched into the thick vinyl seatback.

There was only enough room for two people to sit beside his desk. The rest of the space was jammed with abandoned file cabinets, worn-out chairs, stacks of newspapers. Bookshelves behind him sagged under the weight of their heavy, dusty volumes.

I said to Happy, "So, what the Hell are *you* doing here?"

Happy nodded toward a couple of my gym friends a few feet away. He stood about six-two with a flattop buzz cut and a Glock G20 Short Frame beneath his jacket. He said, "Those guys found him. Didn't know how to report it. Looks like a heart attack."

I looked across; Mike and Jesse stood off to the side, uncertain about what they should be doing.

Happy added, "Unexplained death; we got here as soon as we could. I didn't want anyone contaminating the scene. Like you."

Lt. Ralph "Happy" Moynihan and I had had more run-ins than either of us liked. It was his cop buddies who christened him with the Happy moniker because he never seemed to be—happy—and because his real name was Ralph.

"So, you knew him well?" he asked.

"Yeah, you could say that."

"Care to elaborate?"

I asked, "What have you got so far?"

"You're seeing it. Their call came in at ten; we were just around the corner." Happy raised his voice a notch and appealed to the crime scene technician that examined Jack's eyes and status of rigor mortis. "So, Ted, time of death?"

The guy spoke without looking over. "Hour ago."

If you didn't know where to look for the vintage timepiece in the overloaded office, you wouldn't have noticed it. The hands of the round Sinclair Oil clock in a corner pointed to 10:30 a.m.

God, Jack. What the Hell happened? You never saw a doctor in your life; you never missed a day at the gym. You're the personification of health and strength. You're ... Jack.

I stepped toward Mike and Jesse. Friends of mine across the years from working out in the gym, they both worked at FDNY. The two sat on a couple of benches covered with red metal-flake vinyl held together by grey duct tape.

"I'm sorry you had to find him," I said.

Jesse hung his head. He couldn't speak. I liked Jesse; I turned to Mike.

Mike grimaced a non-smile and nodded his head, weighted with sorrow.

"What can you tell me?" I asked.

Happy approached us. "Look, Wolfe, I know you and the guy were friends, but don't interfere with police business."

I didn't grimace. I didn't shoot him a mean stare. I just looked at Lt. Moynihan with the calmest, most detached non-expression I had in my repertoire. That scared him worse. "Scram," I said. "I'm talking to my friends."

Happy, wasn't. But he read my signals and made the wise decision to step aside. He said, "I don't get paid enough to deal with the likes of you."

"Maybe you should find another job," I said.

I didn't like the way he looked at me. He replied, "Don't tempt me," and turned back to his crime-scene team.

I turned back to Mike. "What gives?"

"I don't know," he said. "We came in when we got off our shift this morning. He was lying there. Like that."

Jack opened six mornings a week at 8:00 a.m. I arrived with the regular crowd that matriculated around 10:00. The numbers grew through the day into the evening until he closed up shop at 8:00 p.m.

I wanted to sit with him, be with him. But not like this. Not with a veteran crew of disinterested CSI professionals that inspected his office and his mortal remains, zipped him up in a body bag, called it a day, and stopped off for some rotgut at a watering hole before they went home from work.

I knew that was their job, but it wasn't mine. I wanted to be with Jack, his spirit. I looked up, stared at the ceiling and had a feeling I already was.

Minutes before when I stood beneath the rain rivulets outside, my capacity for decisions was overrun with ponderous questions. This dropped another big one on top of them. Both quarreling angels on my opposite shoulders called a temporary truce. They agreed: "Let's get out of here."

That was my last training session at Jack's. I felt uncomfortable. I wanted to clean out my locker, get out of there, go home—*wherever the Hell that was.*

I walked around the desk, behind my friend. Out of habit, I took care not to scrape my back against his thumbtacked *objets d'art.* Curled from age and sunlight they hung, folded, spindled, and mutilated on the walls of the tight space: postcards, letters, photos with friends.

And magazine spreads. Jack's office had become a minor gallery of major models. They checked in from seven continents and rented the landmark sweatshop for glossy magazine photo shoots. On any given Saturday morning the scenery in Jack's Gym improved in dramatic fashion.

Scantily clad tanned and taut beauties juxtaposed their smooth, lithe, bodies against the rough, raw, décor. Some of the gatefolds on the walls of his inner chancery sparked adolescent conversations among us middle-aged men.

The M.E. crew and Happy permitted me the courtesy of a final moment. I wanted to say goodbye, laid my hand on Jack's back one last time.

A moment later, I said, "Happy, I'm glad you're here."

"I'm flattered," came his sarcastic reply. "Why?"

"Because if he died of a heart attack, it was induced." I grabbed Jack's black T-shirt at his waist and yanked it up over his shoulders.

"Hey!" said the lieutenant. "You can't ..."

He stopped when he saw it: a red dot on the left side of Jack's back, behind his heart. There was no blood. The soft red puncture wound made the area around it feel hard at the source, then mushy around it.

He leaned forward for a closer look. Happy's fingertips gently pressed the penetration trauma around the wound. "No hesitation marks," he said.

The roll of my eyes was involuntary. "I don't think he poked around before he stabbed himself in the back, Happy."

The lieutenant ignored my comment. "Icepick," he said. "No laceration drainage."

I felt my body tense, my jaws tighten. "Shivved from behind," I said. "A pro. He used some kind of blood arrester to minimize the bleeding." I drew in deep breaths through my nose because my jaws were clenched so tight it felt like my teeth would crack.

I said, "The CIA learned that trick from the Mafia. When they do an autopsy and he lies on his back, a lot of times they don't even see the puncture wound that caused the heart attack."

Happy said, "Had to be somebody he knew. They shouldn't be hard to find. That register over there lists everyone who's been here today."

I said, "Sure, it does. It lists me, too, but I just got here. You think the killer signed in? Maybe he smashed a clean set of fingerprints just to be certain. Come on, Ralph. You're better than that."

Happy's eyes squinted. He ground his teeth. "I don't like you, Wolfe. Never have. I don't like your cowboy attitude; I don't like that ridiculous arsenal you carry, and I don't like how the White House covers for you."

He got so wound up he had difficulty finding his words. "You're a mediocre p.i., that ... God knows how you got your license. And now you've become some kind of media darling. You've got to be the luckiest son-of-a-bitch alive."

"Somebody up there likes me," I said.

"It's no ancestor of mine," he muttered beneath his breath.

Then he detonated again. "Screw you! You back into things; they fall into your lap, and you come out a hero. How the Hell you married Electra White ... so you live with the wealthiest woman in the world—

wait, just a minute. What *are* you doing here? Aren't you supposed to be..."

One of the CSI team nudged Happy. He scribbled his signature on a form. Without looking up he asked, "Aren't you supposed to be at the White House today?"

"Tomorrow," I said. Then, "Maybe."

"What do you mean, *maybe*?"

I looked at Jack's body across his desk. "Something came up," I said.

* * *

Back cover copy for Assassination Attempt!

Nick Wolfe's friend Jack is murdered. His wife, Electra, wants him to move from Manhattan to D.C.; his sister, Trouble, moves to L.A.; the First Lady puts him on furlough from F.L.O.T.U.S.; and his Lower East Side home is blown to rubble ... yet he vows to nail Jack's killer.

Meanwhile, two assassination attempts on the President have failed.

The media screams: Will there be a third?

On Saturday, July 4, 2026, the day of America's sestercentennial anniversary, POTUS will speak to America and the world, live, from the base of the Statue of Liberty.

It's an election year and the biggest day in American history since our 1976 bicentennial. The opposition will do anything to stop President John T. Jackson.

What could possibly go wrong?

Can Nick Wolfe save America?

LOST AND FOUND

Shann Tajiah

So much to say.
No words to say it
While fear and hope
Mingle
In a confusing whirl
Of anger

(You're not the only one
Afraid of destroying
I'm not the only one
Who could be destroyed)

Take me back to the start
To the warmth of infatuation
Before jokes sharpened somehow
To a razor's edge.
Before the purposeful
Misunderstandings
Took root.

(I'm not the only one
Feeling so lost.
You're not the only one
Feeling found at the same time)

I ASKED

A Short Story by Linda Gordon

Stepping carefully into the waning moonlight, I cautiously test the ice layering the old plank porch, then head purposefully toward the shadowy outline of the barn. I silently count the steps, as I do every morning, from the porch to the well, from the well to the barn. Even in that short distance my eyes adjust quickly to the dark, but I don't look to my right when I reach twenty-seven steps, the distance to the well. I know it is there even if the wind is still and there is no creaking of rope or sighing through the rocks surrounding it. Another twenty-seven steps lead me right to the door of the barn. I wonder if the steps will still be the same when I turn twelve in three months, or if I will grow so much before then that the number will change with my stride. Even now I know that my pants are getting shorter on me. No one else seems to notice them inching towards the tops of my boots.

A wave of pungent smells washes over me as I push open the barn door and feel for the lantern hanging on the wall. I light it quickly before shutting out the moonlight and keeping in the warmth from the three cows that stand waiting to be milked. Bossy turns her head and rolls her eyes to the side as she snorts a greeting. I know she is asking to be milked first, as she does every morning. Mama named her Bossy because she liked to push her way to the front even as a calf. Mama laughed when she named her, but I think she secretly likes her best. Once, when Bossy got separated from the other cows, she cried and cried until Mama put them back together. When I said she should have named her Cry Baby, Mama replied thoughtfully, "Luke, sometimes it is okay to ask for what you want, even over and over."

I quickly fork some hay into the feed trough, then place my hand on Bossy's back, gently stroking as I set the bucket under her. She shifts to her other leg as I sit and lean my forehead against her side and begin to milk. I close my eyes and think about Mama, as I have every morning since she left. The fall air was sharp then, snapping the brittle leaves off the oak trees behind the house. Mama first started to cough every night, then during the day as well. I would ask her if she needed me to gather wild sassafras that grew in the thorny hollow to make tea, and she would nod and tell me I was a good son. When she grew weaker, the doctor came. After examining her, he and Pa stepped outside to talk quietly. Pa just stood on the porch after he left, watching the dust settle back onto the road. I wanted to be like Bossy and ask Pa to do something to make Mama well, but the look on his face made something inside me hurt, and I just went to sit by her instead.

A week later, we got a telegram saying that Mama's brother was coming to visit. I had never met my Uncle Robert. Mama had told me stories about him, though. She says that I remind her of him with my rusty red hair. He is three years older than Mama and wasn't afraid of anything when they were growing up. Her favorite story to tell is when he grabbed Grandma's Sunday dress off the clothes line and used it to beat a rattlesnake that had been hiding under the porch. He left the farm when he was sixteen and ended up working for the railroad. Mama said he lives in a fine house now, in Boston.

On Friday, Pa went to pick Uncle Robert up at the train station. I was curious to see what someone who wasn't afraid of anything would look like. He looked ordinary to me, but he had a booming voice that seemed to come from deep in his chest when he talked. It wasn't until Uncle Robert got here that Pa told me that he had come to take Mama back East with him to stay in a special hospital while she got well. Pa's mouth smiled when he told me, but his eyes looked so sad that I wished even more that I was like Bossy and could ask Uncle Robert to not take her away, but I couldn't get the words past my lips.

The next morning, I was sent to the well to draw water for breakfast. I had tried to sleep that night, but every time Mama coughed, I would feel a fear rise up in my chest. I felt as if I were suffocating, wondering if Mama would get well, if she would come back home. Tears I had been holding back began to run down my cheeks as I dropped the bucket into the well. The tears fell faster, and for a wild minute I wondered if I would fill the well to the top with them before I could stop. When I finally looked up and lifted my sleeve to wipe my nose, I saw Uncle Robert standing a little way off watching me. Shame washed over me. I was crying like a baby in front of the man who was not afraid of anything. Uncle Robert walked over to stand beside me and gently laid his hand on my shoulder. His booming voice was quiet as he spoke, like the rumble of thunder in the distance after a storm.

"Luke, there are all kinds of bravery in this world. The bravest men are not the ones who put themselves in danger but the ones who face their greatest fear."

When they left that morning, Uncle Robert first shook Pa's hand and then mine, as if I were already grown. I hugged Mama for a long moment and whispered, "I'll take care of Pa," before letting go. When I went to milk that night and leaned my head against Bossy's side, I finally knew who I could ask for what I wanted. Every morning and evening since then, I have prayed for God to bring Mama back home. Her letters say she is getting stronger.

I hurry to finish milking when I see the sun peeking through the cracks in the barn. Stepping outside, I begin to count the steps to the well. As I get closer, my steps slow. Overnight, the crocuses Mama had planted around the well have pushed shoots up through the slushy snow. I know it will only be a few days before they bloom their sunny yellow. I take a deep breath and smell the wet earth. Spring is coming, and Mama will soon be home. She will be happy to see me and Pa and even Bossy. She will notice how tall I have gotten, and I will hug her and tell her how I asked and asked, just like Bossy.

THE RIPPLES OF LEGACY

An inspirational article by S.T. Arriaga

What does it mean to leave a legacy? Too often, we think of legacy as something huge and earth shaking, world-changing deeds, fame, or influence that we hope will stretch far into the future after we are gone. But the truth is, if we consider the forks in the roads of our lives, and the people that have influenced and changed our trajectory, legacy is not always measured the way we think it is. Sometimes it's measured in a moment with a stranger, the lives we touch, and the words we preserve, or the truths that we dare to record.

I began to consider this idea of legacy when I learned of the passing of someone I knew only briefly, but I will always remember vividly: Dr. Duane Hale. He leaves behind a great legacy, and it isn't one just of personal achievement, though his list of accomplishments is long and remarkable. He was an athlete, a scholar, a professor, a museum director, a prolific writer, and a passionate seeker of history and truth. He spent decades teaching and preserving history-most notably the tribal histories of over 500 Native American communities across the U.S. and Canada. His passion and dedication ensured that voices which might have otherwise been lost and forgotten were preserved for future generations. Through research and teaching, he didn't just record history, he equipped others to preserve their own.

But beyond his vast achievements, Dr. Hale's legacy lives in the lives he touched. His influence rippled outward from the classroom, workshops, writing club meetings, and bookshelves into the hearts and minds of students, colleagues, and friends. He brought history to life, and his passion was infectious. He was the living embodiment of heart meeting scholarship, which created recognition that every life, every culture, every voice matters.

My fondest memory of Dr. Hale was when I had volunteered to give a workshop about creating an author bio. It was an unfortunate night, in that most of our group had prior commitments, and Dr. Hale was the only person that came to the meeting. At the time, I was devastated, but I have an interest in Native American history and Dr. Hale liked what he called, "your intelligent questions". We ended up talking for hours about Native American history and his experiences working with tribes to teach them how to create a written history to preserve an oral history that was fading into the past.

When Dr. Hale first began working with the tribes, he didn't expect it to grow the way it did. He was just following his passion and his interest and through that he found his path and his calling on this earth. I believe that this is where our true legacy begins – with our passions, our interests, and throwing our heart into what we love. That kind of energy catches like a fire sometimes or just lights a spark in someone – and it changes everything, even when we don't see it in the now.

As authors and people, we may never know the full impact of our lives in the same way that Dr. Hale was able to see how his work impacted so many over the years. Some of us may write books that shift national conversations, give us a public platform, or help change lives in real-time. Others of us may pen a story, a poem, or an essay that quietly transforms a single belief, or impacts a single life. Both matter. Both leave marks that outlive us and change perspectives for the future.

Dr. Hale's life reminds me that legacy isn't just about how many people know your name. It's about how many lives are better because you were here, because you were kind to someone, because you took the time to write, to share, to teach, to bless, or preserve. Our words and our daily interactions with others are threads, weaving connections across generations. One day, long after we're gone, someone may come across our words and find strength, healing, or hope.

That is the mark that we make as authors. That is the mark we leave as human beings. And one day, like Dr. Hale, I hope to leave a legacy of passion, perseverance, and giving voices to the voiceless. I hope my life is a ripple that continues outward through time, even when my name is long forgotten.

CLOSER TO THE START

Roma Johnson Holley

When we are closer to the end than we are at the start
When time has finally slowed the beating of our heart
When our eyes begin to dim and our breath begins to slow
Our peace comes from within because we already know

That the end is really a beginning.
It's the last step of a race that we are winning.
We are tired from the struggles of our full but happy life.
We long to be free from the ever-present strife.

A new day will soon dawn and we'll walk along the shore
Of the River of Life with those who've gone before.
With the sun in my eyes and The Son of God holding my hand
My life will begin with Him in the promised land.

So don't cry for me just let me slip away
And know that I will see you again on that beautiful day.
Don't cry as this old body gives up its tired heart.
Be thankful that now I am closer to the start.

ABOUT THE AUTHORS

PRISCILLA BETTIS

Priscilla Bettis is an avid reader and a joyful writer. Priscilla lives in small-town Texas with her two-legged and four-legged family members. She enjoys writing short stories and poems inspired by her awe of God and love for fellow human beings.

Priscilla is a multiple Cisco Writers Club Annual Writing Contest winner. "Hurry Every Chance You Get" won first place in the 2023 Articles category. "Fix Your Face" won first place in the 2024 Short Stories category.

The poem "Love in the Dark" is included in Priscilla's upcoming collection, *Whispers of a Southern Moon*, to be released fall 2025.

Priscilla is a reviewer at The Well Read Fish, a Christian fiction review blog: https://thewellreadfish.com. She chats about life and writing on X: https://x.com/PriscillaBettis.

BRIAN CALLARMAN

Brian Callarman is an author of historical fiction whose primary interest is exploring the lives of individuals caught in the shifting tides of empires and cultural conflict. *Of Those Dead* won First Place in the 2022 Cisco Writers Club Annual Writing Contest (books category) as well as the Mary Carey Award for the best fiction book. The story revolves around the complex relationship between a displaced Pawnee woman and a violent criminal. The two knew each other as children, and now they must depend on one another to navigate the treacherous world of the pre-Civil War American West.

Brian recently retired from a career as a Parole Officer and is now focused on writing. As an avid reader and student of history, he is particularly drawn to stories where the historical record is incomplete—where imagination might fill in what has been lost. His current project, *False Hearted Nations*, focuses on 18th century piracy in the lawless Caribbean as seen through the eyes of an escaped Jamaican slave. Over the years, Brian has published magazine articles about elk hunting and conservation, and his fiction has won or placed in several writing contests.

Brian lives in Montana with his wife and three kids. When he's not researching archaic maritime slang, he enjoys hunting, fly-fishing, and hiking in the magnificent Rocky Mountains.

HELEN COZART

After spending twenty years in the Army as an Intelligence Analyst, Helen Cozart retired to become a History Professor and taught at both Cisco College and Dallas College part time. Always looking for something closer to home and full-time, she stumbled into the library at Ranger College and never left. She considers it to be the last job she will ever have. Being a librarian had never occurred to her, but it turned out to be the fusion of all the aspects she loved of all her previous experiences—analysis, research, teaching, and helping students.

Helen Cozart uses social media for professional purposes, including writing a weekly blog on using AI in academia: https://library.rangercollege.edu/blogs/what-about-ai. She does not participate in personal social media, but does maintain a portfolio through the Ranger College Library website. You can view her previous works at https://library.rangercollege.edu/helenportfolio.

Helen's "The Tragic Story of Byron Parrish" is a nonfiction narrative and a written version of a 2022 oral presentation at the West Texas Historical Association annual meeting.

STEVE DENEHAN

Steve Denehan lives in Kildare, Ireland, with his wife Eimear and daughter Robin. He is the award-winning author of two chapbooks and seven poetry collections. Denehan's "Salt and Vinegar," "Mount Carmel Maternity Ward, January 2012," and "The Summer Blurs By Outside" are all winning poems in Cisco Writers Club's Annual Writing Contests. "Dust and Stones," "Remembering—A Poem about Dementia," and "Shooting Stars" are all new poems in *Golden Nuggets.*

Find Steve online at:

https://stevedenehanpoetry.com

https://twitter.com/SteverinoD

https://www.facebook.com/denehan

https://www.instagram.com/steverinod/

https://bsky.app/profile/steverinod.bsky.social

LINDA GORDON

I've always liked writing, but it was put on hold until I retired from teaching. Since then, I have had short stories published in *Christian Woman* magazine and poetry in other venues. I have found my joy in writing for various contests and in gifts and requested writings for family and friends. My writing goal and desire is to be a wordsmith, making words my signature art, fashioned from the heart, and to give Glory where Glory is due.

I have no social media venues.

Other writings have placed in the Cisco Writers Club Writing Contest, but the writings I chose to submit for the *Golden Nuggets* anthology are "I Asked" which won first place in 2015 for Short Story, "The Rock" which won third place in 2016 for Articles and also won the Lou Prange Inspiration Award for Highest Ranking Article of Inspiration, and "Dream Vacation" which won first place in 2017 for Publication Briefs and also won the Julia B. Worthy Columns Award.

THANK YOU for your annual contests and continual promotion and encouragement for writing and writers.

ROMA JOHNSON HOLLEY

Roma Holley was born and raised in West Texas and grew up loving animals and all things country. She was taught to love the Lord and seek His guidance in all things. Her life was enriched as she traveled to and lived in several countries and states, and she encountered many people who helped influence and refine her love of God. As a mother of four and grandmother of six, she tries to set an example for her children and grandchildren so that their paths will lead to eternal life with God the Father.

Roma is the current Vice President of the Cisco Writers Club. Her piece, Texas Drawl, received 3rd place in the Inspirational category in the 2025 Annual Cisco Writers Contest.

J.V. LEWIS

J.V. is the second of three children whose parents are Roy and Mattie (Fenter) Lewis. Born January 27, 1938, J.V. grew up as a son of farmers until his parents bought a Help-Your-Self Laundry business in Carbon, Texas, when he was fourteen years old. That move took him from grade school in DeLeon, Texas, to Carbon when he was in the eighth grade.

He continued the remainder of his formal education until he graduated from Carbon High School in the spring of 1957. Upon graduation, he entered the work force taking his first significant job as a factory worker for Boss Manufacturing Company which manufactured canvas and leather work gloves.

Prior to his graduation, he had met the young lady who would later become his wife for 65 years and counting. J.V. and his wife, Nada (Beard) Lewis, now live in Eastland, Texas, and are delighted to have three adult children, nine grandchildren, fourteen great-grandchildren, and one great-great grandson.

J.V. left his job as a factory worker to enter the field of construction in 1963. After working as a carpenter's helper for a brief period of time, he joined the Commercial Carpenter's Union in Dallas, Texas, and retired from the union as a journeyman carpenter in 2000.

He worked in many high-rise buildings in Dallas and Fort Worth in addition to the Texas Stadium for the Dallas Cowboys in Irving, Texas, in 1971. The Dallas Cowboys have now built a new Stadium; the original one was imploded several years ago.

After retirement, J.V. and Nada lived in Gainesville, Texas, for a few years until Nada suffered a stroke on Thanksgiving Day of 2015. After spending some time in ICU, first in Plano then in Sherman, she was taken to a Nursing and Rehab Center in Eastland in January of 2016. She is now a resident at The Woodlands in Eastland.

Since Nada has been in rehab, J.V. wrote a book, *Knowing Our Savior,* in 2016, became an Uber driver in Abilene in 2017, worked as a pizza deliver for Pizza Hut in Eastland in 2018, became a driver for Blake Fullenwider in Eastland until mid 2019, and then took a job working for ResCare where he worked until 2022.

Upon leaving his job at ResCare, he started an online business. After spending a substantial amount of time on it, he decided to turn it over to someone else and become fully retired again. Presently, he pays daily visits to The Woodlands to see Nada. He and the residents enjoy playing Bingo and Dominoes every day.

J.V. has purchased a handicap van so he can give Nada a chance to get out and go shopping and go to the home J.V. bought in 2019. The van also enables him to take her to her doctors' appointments even when they are out of town.

Learn more about J.V.'s book *Knowing Our Savior* at https://www.amazon.com/dp/B094YVV8NR/

JENNIFER NEVILLE MADDLE

After a substantial number of years as a high school English teacher, Jennifer Maddle retired and tried to become a writer, purely for the pleasure of it. She continues to live in a small town in Texas with her adoring and long-suffering husband Bud and a house full of pets. Most days she can be found listening to gangster rap music or pursuing her love of interpretive dance, and sometimes both at the same time.

Her short story "The Billy Budd Incident or The Handbasket Express" was awarded first place honor in the 46th Annual Cisco Writers Club Writing Contest in September of 2022. Her "mostly true" memoir, *The Handbasket Express*, was published in May of 2024. She is currently at work on her yet-to-be-titled second book. Follow her on Facebook at Scribbles by Jennifer Neville Maddle https://www.facebook.com/people/Scribbles-by-Jennifer-Neville-Maddle/61558600820977/ for more information and current updates.

ROBERT ROBESON

Robert Robeson's short story "A Hootch Maid's Farewell Letter" won first place in the Cisco Writers Club 44th Annual Writing Contest. Robeson's article "An Infantry Medic I'll Remember Forever" won first place in the Cisco Writers Club 46th Annual Writing Contest. And his short story "A Valentine for Vinny" won first place in the Cisco Writers Club 47th Annual Writing Contest. Fifty-three of his other short stories, poems, and articles have also placed in CWC contests. He's been awarded the CWC David Autry Sweepstakes prize five times and has tied for it once. He's been published over 980 times in 330 publications in 130 countries and 81 anthologies. This includes *Reader's Digest, Writer's Digest, Vietnam Combat, Soldier of Fortune,* and *Positive Living*, among others. He retired from the US Army after 27 years of service and while flying as a "Dustoff," a medical evacuation helicopter pilot in the Vietnam War. Recently, he was awarded a US Congressional Gold Medal (along with his Dustoff compatriots) for their critical actions during combat. He has a BA in English from the University of Maryland, College Park, and has completed extensive undergraduate and graduate work in journalism at the University of Nebraska, Lincoln. He's also been awarded fifteen George Washington Honor Medals for articles and speeches on freedom from the Freedoms Foundation at Valley Forge, Pennsylvania. Robeson retired in Lincoln, Nebraska, with his wife, Phyllis, of 56 years.

LINDA SPETTER, PH.D.

Linda Spetter is a Professor of English and Communication at Cisco College. Since 2013, she has been teaching the same subjects at Cisco that she taught for 17 years at a university in Japan (American Literature, English Composition, Mass Communication, and Journalism). She also does folklore research. Linda is a former newspaper editor and is a member of the Texas Folklore Society as well as the Western States Folklore Society. "The Case of the Skeletal Remains of a Texas Ranger Lost on the Battlefield of Eskota" was originally published as a guest column in the Abilene Reporter-News in the mid-1970s in Katharyn Duff's "Page One" column.

SHANN TAJIAH/S.T. ARRIAGA

Shann is a Minnesota-grown-Texan, award winning poet, author, and photographer. Her love for words began at age four when she taught herself to read from the newspaper, and at age eight she discovered the joy of crafting stories and poems of her own. She shares her heart and imagination through stories about redemption, healing, and love, whether through poetry or stories about worlds far beyond the stars.

Shann is the author of the *East of Eeden* series, along with *Scraps of Love: Poetry from the Darkest Night 1997-2010*, and *The Author Platform Roadmap*, which was born from a class she taught at the Cisco Writers Club. Her latest work, *Sacred Renewal: Embracing the Biblical Design for Self-Care* marks her first release under her alternate penname, S.T. Arriaga.

Her passion for authors and publishing led her to found Ithirial Rising Press and Kadesh Ink Author Services, where she offers coaching and support for fellow authors on their own paths of creative discovery.

Shann lives in West Central Texas with her husband, their crazy dog, Frolic, and easygoing cat, Jakob. Beyond the pen, Shann enjoys cooking, spending time outdoors, daydreaming in her hammock, and all things music. She is also the current President of the Cisco Writers Club.

The Shaloma is the recipient of the 2021 Cisco Writers Contest First in Fiction and the Mary Carey Award.

The Rooster was created at a Cisco Writers Club flash-fiction workshop.

You can follow Shann's journey on YouTube and Facebook @authorshanntajiah and at www.shanntajiah.com

SHANE TOVAR

Shane lee von Tover loves reading books with horror, science fiction, and mystery, and he's watched the SYFY channel on TV since he was a little boy. Now, he wants to create his own stories like no one has ever read before, and he hopes you enjoy them.

JIM WILSON

Jim Wilson grew up on an irrigated farm/ranch combination 12 miles south of Van Horn, Texas. He graduated from high school in 1968. He is a retired veterinarian having practiced in Abilene for 42 years after graduating from the veterinary school at Texas A&M in 1973.

Jim and his wife moved to a place east of Burton in August 2015. They have cows, chickens, goats, and a garden.

Jim began writing poetry in 2000. He doesn't know exactly what qualifies one to be a poet, but his best explanation is that there is a poetic muse that chooses to walk with some people. It directs one's observation and intuition to record messages that turn out to be poems in Jim's case. He knows this sounds corny, but it's the best he can do. Jim only knows that the poems do not come from him. They come through him.

Jim has published six poetry books and has several publishing credits including *Concho River Review, The Mountain Spirit, Ft. Davis Mountain Dispatch, San Antonio Express-News, The Desert Candle, Border Senses* (a publication associated with University of Texas at El Paso), *Cenizo, Abilene Stories: From Then to Now, Window Cat Press, Civilized Beasts II, Poetic Bond* (issues VIII, IX, and X), 2021 and 2022 *Texas Poetry Calendar, Front Porch Magazine,* and *The Big Bend Literary Journal.*

He recently had two poems chosen to be included in the *Robert Indiana: A Legacy of Love* exhibit at the McNay Art Museum in San Antonio.

Jim won the North Texas Book Festival Book Award for best poetry book for *Down to Earth Poetry*. He was nominated for a Pushcart Prize and was a finalist for the Writers League of Texas's Violet Crown Book Award for prose and poetry. Jim was a presenter at the 2017 *Langdon Review of the Arts* poetry weekend. He had a poem chosen for the 2020 VIA Metropolitan Transit's Poetry on the Move contest.

Jim Wilson's "Urban Renewal" poem won Honorable Mention in the 2020 Cisco Writers Club Annual Writing Contest, and his "First Responder" poem won First Place in the 2021 Contest.

ROB WITHERSPOON

Rob Witherspoon was born and raised in rural Texas. He earned a BA in Physical Education, UT Arlington, 1985, and a BS in Aerospace Engineering, UT Arlington, 1990. He lives in North Central Texas with his wife and youngest daughter and has spent much of his life in rural communities and on the ranch.

"The Feed Sack Tote" won First Place in the Articles category as well as Best Nostalgia Article in the 2016 Cisco Writers Club Annual Writing Contest.

Find Rob online at:

https://www.robwitherspoon.com

https://bsky.app/profile/roobwiddershins.bsky.social

ROBERT WORKMAN

Robert writes books for guys who like to read books. Read the reviews—ladies like them even more.

Here's why:

A sprinter/hurdler on the UT Austin track team, Robert has always enjoyed speed. He has driven six of his Ferraris in cross-Texas races. At the Bootlegger Run, a 1,200 cross-Texas road rally, he and his navigator received the trophy for "Best Team."

But that isn't what's important right now ...

What's important is that he writes stories like he drives. Jump into one of his books with him. Race through his noir action novels. You'll feel like you're driving west out of Dallas at 135 mph, late to a Diana Krall concert at the Fort Worth Bass Hall—with no tickets. (That happened.)

At age 27, he was recruited and interviewed by the CIA in their Langley, Virginia, offices, then at a hotel in Austin, Texas. He told them they didn't pay enough money and flew home. They probably called everyone into the office, broke out the Jim Beam, and had a party.

If you want to hang out with a guy who is given to exotic cars, mountain lions for house pets in his downtown warehouse home, and a West Texas cattle ranch writing residence, check out one of his books.

Robert tells people at his book signings, "You may love it, you may hate it, but I guarantee you will be entertained."

Maximum Prejudice—Amazon #1 Best Selling Political Thriller

Immigration Invasion!—Amazon #1 Best Selling Political Thriller

Assassination Attempt!—Coming Soon!

Robert's short story "Hooked" won first place in the 2025 Cisco Writers Club Writing Contest, and his novel *Assassination Attempt!* won honorable mention in the books category.

Find Robert Workman online at robert-workman.com.

RUTH V. YORK

Ruth V. York is still deciding what she wants to be when she grows up. But in the meantime she has been some pretty wonderful things: worker, wife, mother. Kitchen chemist. Occasional artist. Educator to her eight children.

Ruth is blessed to live on the farm where she grew up. Always captivated by the written word, she was delighted to discover the Cisco Writers Club in 1986. Ruth values the Cisco Writers Club in part for the remarkable people one meets there, and for the fascinating stories they share.

On a trek to Minnesota one summer with husband Joe, their children, and Joe's mother (also Ruth York), Ruth passed the time repeating tales written by Cisco Writers Club members. "You know the most interesting people!" her mother-in-law exclaimed. One such person was Patrick Ready. He often challenged his fellow writers with quirky prompts like this one: Develop three fictional characters placed in West Texas, in the vicinity of Fort Davis or the McDonald Observatory, with the common occupations of butcher, baker, and candlestick maker. Ruth's story "Grit" is the result.

Most of Ruth's writing is utilitarian—letters, newsletters, press releases and such—but she enjoys writing songs and exploring fiction as well.

Ruth V. York now serves as Treasurer and Contest Director of Cisco Writers Club.

Made in the USA
Coppell, TX
10 February 2026